D1385179

Remember No More

Rem

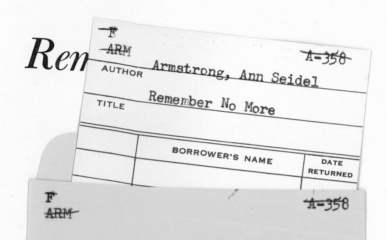

F
ARM   A-358
AUTHOR   Armstrong, Ann Seidel

TITLE   Remember No More

	BORROWER'S NAME	DATE RETURNED

NIHIL OBSTAT:
John F. Murphy, S.T.D.
Censor librorum

IMPRIMATUR:
✠ William E. Cousins
Archbishop of Milwaukee

July 22, 1963

Library of Congress Catalog Card Number: 63-21346

To the memory of
EMORY P. SEIDEL, *sculptor*

AUTHOR'S NOTE

THE principal events in this story actually occurred, bloody and dreadful, yet shot through with brilliance and heroism. Across the distance of space and time, the events still stand out sharp and clear, and even the background can be filled in with patient research. But the hopes and fears and thoughts of the people are buried deep in the dust and shards of a city that no longer exists.

The ideas that were in conflict at that time we know and the paths that men followed in their pursuit, crossing, joining, or coming in opposition to one another. But an idea confronted in this way always wears a face, sometimes the face of the one we know best, sometimes the face of the one who first showed us its substance; sometimes the face is a composite, or it changes, but it never becomes completely amorphous, it tends to cling to personality. The faces in this account can only be sketched in with conjecture and colored with imagination, for it all happened a very long time ago, and no one can say with truth that this is how or why it happened and no one can say that it is not.

Remember No More

THE city was Carthage, the capital of the Roman province of Africa, a vast territory extending all the way from the boundary of Egypt in the east to the Strait of Gibraltar in the west. Carthage had had a turbulent history, from being tyrannical mistress of the western Mediterranean Sea to total destruction by the armies of the Roman Republic. But now in the beginning of the third century of the Empire, Carthage was a prosperous, crowded metropolis which had benefited from Roman administration and business to such an extent that it now enjoyed a sounder economy than it had ever known in the time of its independence.

The peninsula of Carthage hooks into the Mediterranean Sea, a natural haven baited with a pleasant equable climate and the rich produce of the coastal lowlands. From the beginning it caught those traveling from east to west, its trader-founders from Phoenicia speaking the Punic tongue, artists and artisans from Greece, Jewish and Asiatic weavers and dyers, Christians also at a later date. At this time the predominantly Eastern character of its inhabitants was overlaid by a veneer of Latinism. A togaed crowd thronged the forum and Latin was spoken everywhere, but many a "Roman" when jostled would swear in Punic.

About one hundred thousand people were crowded into the narrow lowlands between the sea and the lake of Tunis, and another hundred thousand more graciously situated in the large suburb of Megara which filled out the peninsula. Carthage was perched on the very northernmost part of Africa, harsh, austere, aloof, as if she would preserve herself free from the wildness of the vast continent. Her smiles were only for those who approached from the sea. To them she revealed a single imposing height crowned with majestic temples and public buildings. As one entered the harbor one could see streets lined with fine homes and apartment buildings, many built five and six stories high to conserve space. The farther one went south from the sea and the harbors and the closer to the great mass of Africa, the poorer the homes and the poorer the people. Near the pestilential marshes by the lake there lived in direst poverty and subject to periodic epidemics a large colony of people whose hands were red-purple from laboring in the dye works. These slums could not be seen from the two man-made harbors, however, and the buildings and seawalls surrounding them were kept spotless and in excellent repair, for this was the lifeline of Carthage and the channel for the granary of Rome.

From the harbors a short wide avenue, the only wide street in Carthage, led to the marketplace, where it opened into a busy square, and then continued on to end in the forum. Down the whole length of the Via Septimia could be seen the magnificent fountain in the center of the forum which had been completed by the emperor in the beginning of this year. The base of the fountain formed a reservoir from which the people in the tenements in the city could draw water freely, and to remind them that this bounty was due to Rome, an inscription was cut into the square of gray Numidian marble at the front.

This inscription read:

HAEC.FACT.AUC.CMLVI

A.SEPTIMIO.SEVERO.IMP.X.ANN.

PROCO.MINUCIO.TIMINIANO.

which is translated:

"This was built 956 years from the founding of the city (Rome)
By Septimius Severus in his tenth year as emperor
When Minucius Timinianus was proconsul
(in Carthage)."

There was no monument in Carthage bearing the name of Hilarion, proconsul. It was August, and he had been governor only two months since the death of Minucius. Hilarion passed this fountain every morning on his way to the curia where he listened to the more important cases and passed judgment. The women of the city leaned over the fountain or sat on the edge and gossiped with their friends as they drew water. Sometimes the inscription was hidden by their long gowns, sometimes the children as they played traced the lines with their fingers without understanding. Probably no one in the city ever noticed the inscription except Hilarion, but whether he looked at it or away from it, he knew it was there and it filled him with envy.

There was no monument anywhere in the whole world bearing the inscription AD CCIII — in the year of our Lord 203. Not yet was this inscription engraved immobile on hard stone at the base of public buildings or struck on cold

3

metal to be exchanged for goods whether fine or base. Yet it was unquestionably a year of our Lord, even if only relatively few were aware of it, for their awareness was large — total.

There was a man in Carthage named Saturus, a priest, who was just two mouths from the life and death of Jesus Christ. His grandfather had listened to John on the island of Patmos as he sat and taught on his mountain halfway between heaven and earth. He had come to Carthage and he had brought the words of John with him. His son's son had walked with him, sat with him, and listened to him, and the life of Jesus had to the boy the immediacy and reality of an eyewitness account.

In this year the heavy unmoving stones proclaimed in Rome, in Carthage, and all over the Mediterranean world that Septimius Severus was master of the date. Only on the breath of men was the other date written, blown about on the air, light and elusive, as fragile and as potent as the many-winged, life-bearing fluff of the dandelion.

II

THE sun was blazing hot, this fifteenth day of August, and Balbus was glad he had only one block to walk from the forum to his house. He was tired from the long morning of business but he was chuckling to himself as he came in. He had taken time out on his way from his stall in the marketplace to listen to a student declaiming in high-flown language what was wrong with the world and how he would remedy it. It was amusing to hear the noble ideals and righteous anger of these youths, knowing that in a few short years they would find out, as he had, that money, not thought, held the only substance and power.

But Balbus stopped chuckling when he entered his house, startled and a little dismayed to see a Roman centurion in full armor waiting in the atrium. What in the world could be the matter? Surely his accounts were in perfect order. Balbus was not above cheating on occasion, but never on taxes. The government couldn't prove a thing; he had everything down in black and white. His steward Dion was stumbling and bumbling about, white-faced and shaking, and almost cried with relief when he saw him. He started to stammer out something about soldiers and prisoners, but Balbus silenced him with a gesture and turned to the centurion.

5

Oh, what the deuce! It was Sempronius. He had not recognized him at first. Many an evening they had spent at dice together.

"Well," he said with excessive heartiness, "what can I do for my old friend?"

"You can do me a favor, Balbus," the centurion answered to the merchant's relief. "I have five prisoners in custody next door, and the proconsul doesn't want the arrest known right now. I was instructed to lodge them in a private house temporarily. Do you have an empty room where they could be kept for a day or two? They will be well guarded and the soldiers will have their own rations and provide for the prisoners."

"Prisoners next door?" Balbus' neighbor was an innocuous Greek who had once a thriving business in statues of gods and goddesses but lately had turned to making pots. Unfortunately where he had been a superior craftsman in figures, either from lack of equipment or lack of interest he was remarkably unsuccessful in this new venture. What could he be guilty of, outside of stupidity? "Do you mean Saturninus? What is the charge?"

"I couldn't tell you their names, Balbus, but they were arrested at the potter's shop. They're accused of being Christians. But not a word about it, Balbus, until the proconsul says or it will cost me my rank. Now what about the room?"

Balbus noted the impatience in the centurion's voice and grudgingly conceded to the demand thinly disguised as a request.

"You could use the storeroom off the kitchen, I suppose. I'll show you. There is just the one entrance."

They walked into the court at the back of the house where an ornamental pool, matching the one in the atrium, caught

6

the rainwater from the wide shaft opening to the sky. Next to it and using the same opening for ventilation were a fireplace and ovens now glowing hot from the preparations for dinner. If Balbus had had a wife this large attractive room would have been put to better use and the cooking confined to a small interior room, but in this bachelor establishment the slaves did as they chose in the back of the house as long as their master's rooms were kept clean and comfortable. The confusion in this room was matched only by the accumulation of grease and dirt on the floor and walls. Balbus and the centurion picked their way along the side of the room to a far corner where the merchant pointed out a windowless storage room. The centurion looked in at the small dark room, and a rat scurried behind a large jar in the corner.

"Perfect," he approved. "Not large, but it will do."

Balbus called the steward and directed him to have the wine jars removed from the storeroom.

"Imported, you know, Sempronius," he explained, "from the south of Gaul. I can't abide this Carthaginian wine; it tastes like plaster. I don't dare leave this in with Christians. I heard someone say they actually worship wine! I wouldn't mind that but I'd hate to have them drink it all up for me. Have you time to have a taste of this with me, Sempronius?"

"Not a chance. I must get this business finished, though I think your wine would be quite safe with these prisoners. Two women among them, one far along with child . . . a miserable business. . . . Well, that's neither here nor there. I'll get them at once. And remember, not a word of this and warn your servants too. I'll have their hides if it comes out too soon."

Balbus retired to the atrium to indicate a lack of interest

7

and curiosity, but he managed to notice the prisoners as they were brought in — the two women, as Sempronius had said, both young, one, a Roman matron by her gown, the other who was with child, a slave girl, whose condition did not conceal the unusual beauty and grace of her face and carriage. Small and delicate in feature with dark hair and pale complexion unusual to the Mediterranean countries, she looked fragile beyond belief. The others — his neighbor, Saturninus, and his old father, Secundulus, and last, a rough-looking slave, the only one of the five who could justify even one armed soldier, much less six.

No, Balbus thought, as he stretched out on the couch in relaxation before dinner, his wine would have been safe, unless that one fellow had the capacity of a Polyphemus. But why in the name of Mercury did that fool Saturninus get involved in a sect like this? He had had a marvelous business in statues. Balbus had one of them himself, a beautiful figurine. He had ruined his business completely, and this to Balbus was utterly incomprehensible. For while Balbus admired the statues of gods and goddesses, his only god was business, and the affairs of his life were arranged solely to accommodate its dictates. Even the muscles of his face had disciplined themselves in its service to an enigmatic vacuity the better to disguise the sharpness of the mind behind them. The amassing of money which accompanied his dealings was not an end in itself, it was the manipulation he relished and the stimulus of competition. How his neighbor could throw away his well-earned and productive success for a nebulous attachment to some nebulous deity was beyond his understanding. He shook his head and sighed. A miserable business, indeed. But it was none of his affair, and he had better make sure of that.

III

NIGHT came slowly to the prisoners in the cramped and airless storeroom. The five persons crowded in here had little in common except their language, their faith, and their fear.

They were all from different countries. Only one had been born in Africa. That was the slave girl, and she had been born of a Greek father and a mother who had been a slave since childhood and had forgotten the place of her birth. But it must have been far in the north for her daughter to have such fair skin and clear blue eyes. The girl's name was Felicity, and she was usually sparkling and bright as quicksilver, but now she was heavy with child and her eyes were wide and frightened. She was only sixteen or seventeen years old.

The other woman had come from Rome as a child. She was five years older than Felicity, quiet and serene and madonnalike in her womanhood. She was tall and carried herself proudly, yet her face too showed the strain of keeping her fear held tight within her. This was Vivia Perpetua, Felicity's mistress, and the only Roman among them.

Saturninus, the sculptor, and his father had come from the island of Delos. Both were artists, though Secundulus' hands were too unsteady now to do exact work. He was in his seventies and looked even older. His body was shriveled and bent and his voice shaky. He kept hold of his son's arm and darted worried glances at the open doorway where a soldier paced back and forth.

Saturninus was a small bald man with such a quiet reserved expression that he might be considered gloomy. It was for this reason that his Latin nickname had been given him. Although he and his father were not Roman citizens they had found it useful in business to assume Latin names. Saturninus was undistinguished looking except for his hands, which were very large and restless. He was constantly moving them, plucking at his tunic or pulling at his ear or rubbing and massaging them together. The jerky movements were troublesome to the others because in the vacuity into which they had been thrust, it was the only tangible thing on which to fix their gaze. Yet their stares and the movements themselves were but attempts to erect a barrier against their fear, a barrier as ineffectual as the doorless opening of their prison to the soldiers that stood outside.

The slave whom Balbus had noticed was from Thrace, the mountainous region north of Greece, whose wild and barbarous people had kept apart from the mainstream of civilization and still lived as they had six hundred years ago, before the time of Pericles and Alexander and Caesar. He was a huge muscular man with thick arms and legs and torso and a face that matched the brutishness of his body in ugliness. Thick black hair fell low over his forehead, and that was just as well, for it helped to conceal a dull red "F" for "fugitive" that had been branded there four years ago when he was recaptured after escaping. Perpetua's husband had acquired him at that time and renamed him Revocatus in a kind of jest, because he had been called back from his short taste of freedom. This slave looked as if no brutality would be strange to him, yet for all his massive strength he paced the floor and watched the doorway as tensely and nervously as any of the others.

The room was very still and hot and dark except for a slowly lengthening oblong of glaring sunlight from the open kitchen that cut the little room in half. As the light grew thinner and was finally replaced by the red shadows of the firelight, the room actually seemed less black than it had in the daylight. But they all felt the need for rest, since only by standing and moving about on the empty side of the room had they kept the rats hiding behind the three-foot jars of grain. Even when they had tried to eat the gruel which the soldiers brought them for their dinner they had not cared to sit down.

During the long afternoon the prisoners had conversed in whispers, with their worst fears unspoken, and they made attempts at prayers, but these faltered in their oppression at the dismal surroundings and the uncertainty of their position, for none of the soldiers had spoken a word to them and they did not know whether they would be kept here or taken away at any moment for questioning.

Now when the soldiers had removed the bowl of gruel that served as their dinner and brought a jar of water and another for their night needs, indicating that they were to be undisturbed further, the slave, Revocatus, took the lead in making them comfortable for the night. He gathered up all the old limp rushes that lay on the floor and shook them vigorously on the side of the room where the grain jars were stored. Making a bundle into a crude broom he swept all the grains of wheat and bits of refuse and dirt onto that side,

11

shaking the rushes carefully when he had finished. Then he spread the rushes along the two inner walls. The air was still hot and oppressive, but the stone floor was growing chill and damp from condensation. The inner walls were the driest, and the rushes would give them some protection on the floor.

Gratefully Felicity and Perpetua sat down on the swept floor by the inside wall next to the kitchen. There they could not be seen from the doorway. The opening was like a glaring eye probing their misery, and they longed even for a prison with a heavy locked and barred door to shut out the coarse jests and noisy laughter of the soldiers. At last four of the soldiers left and only two stood guard, so the kitchen became quieter. But the menace remained. . . .

Revocatus uncovered one of the wide-mouthed jars and took out several large handfuls of grain which he placed on the floor in the farthest corner of the room.

"I have to feed our pets, too," he said with a rough attempt at humor. "Let's hope that they won't bother us tonight."

Then he sat down just inside the door next to Felicity, and the bulk of his body there was reassuring to the others. Saturninus and Secundulus sat down by the other wall half-facing the women. They were all silent, the prisoners on the one side and the rats suspiciously peering out from behind the jars. Finally one long black shape disengaged itself from the shadow and approached the grain. Its glittering eyes surveyed the people cautiously, but seeing that they made no movement, the creature began to eat the grain. Then it stopped and glanced back toward the corner and as if by signal another rat and three small ones crept out, not wildly skittering in their usual frantic and fearful rush, but silently with caution rather than fright, and they stayed together at a distance, quietly nibbling the grain.

"Why, it's a little family," laughed Felicity, amazed at the parental care and apparent gentleness of these creatures that filled her with such terror. The remark and the laugh, half-hearted though it was, dissolved some of the tenseness of the little group, held together and yet isolated by the distress and fear they had not voiced.

"I thought there must have been at least twenty of the devils," Saturninus said with a characteristic deprecatory smile.

It was surprising how much the sight of the few rats eating the grain in plain sight without menace had relaxed them all, as if they began to see that they might have exaggerated the rest of their fears equally as much. Perpetua, the Roman matron, especially had held such a tight check on her emotions that the others who by nature and position were more voluble and unrestrained had felt a wall of coldness, which instead of sustaining them, had caused them to retreat the more, each onto his own island of misery. Now as she sat down, she knew by the rush of milk into her breasts that it was time for the night feeding for her baby and she was suddenly overwhelmed by her weariness and pain and her worry for her child.

"Oh, Felicity, what will happen to the baby?" she whispered. "It is more than eight hours since he had anything to eat. There is no one home except Brumilla, and she knows nothing. And besides, what can anyone else do for him? He will starve without me."

"Oh no, mistress, that's not so. A baby can live without his mother or I wouldn't be alive today. Your husband will surely find someone to nurse him in your absence."

13

"That's right," Revocatus added with an abyssmal lack of tact. "He can't stand to hear the baby cry."

"There is no one that is not touched by a baby's distress." Perpetua spoke a little sharply, bridling at the implied criticism. Now she condemned herself for exposing her weakness before these people and she pushed her anxiety into hiding again. "I hope — I'm sure — Novius will be able to find someone to take care of our son. . . ."

"How old is your baby, mistress?" asked the old man, anxious to continue this mood of relaxation. He and the sculptor did not know the others very well, since it was only in the past few months that they had been meeting for instructions in the shop. Before that it was necessary to travel out to the south side where the priest, Saturus, had been able to obtain cheap lodgings. Chiefly to accommodate Perpetua who found it difficult to make such a long trip without arousing suspicion, Saturus had changed the meeting place to the shop near the forum. But they were always pressed for time and had to crowd so many instructions into the meetings that there was no time for social exchange.

"He is seven months old," Perpetua answered, and she smiled for the first time. "Black hair, bright eyes. I think he favors my father. He is gay and quick like my younger brother." She too was bright and lovely when speaking of the baby.

"We have no children," Secundulus said, "that is, I have no grandchildren, but we have children in the house always. Irene is a midwife and often brings a baby home when there is need to find him a nurse or to care for him in sickness. And my son is always modeling one or another of the neighbor children."

14

"Not any more, father. You remember what Saturus said. I haven't made any figures for over a year."

"But what do you think?" Perpetua broke in, hardly listening to the talk of the others, filled with her own thoughts. "Why did the soldiers arrest only the five of us that have not even been baptized? Why didn't they wait for the priest? And why just this one little group?"

Neither of the men answered her directly for truthfully no one did know the answers, but now more questions came from Saturninus, as the gates to their fears and worries were finally lowered. "I wonder how they knew of the meeting place. We have all been very careful. And I am surprised by the suddenness of this arrest. There hasn't been any active persecution for some years. Did you have any inkling of a new policy from your husband, mistress?"

"I have heard nothing," she answered. "But my husband is not at liberty to discuss government affairs at home."

"Perhaps it is the new proconsul," Secundulus added. "He may want to make a show of his power at the expense of a group that the people are readily inflamed against."

"There I find the secrecy encouraging," Saturninus put in, "and the fact that just we five were seized. It doesn't look like a play on mass hysteria. Besides, there has been no trouble recently to blame on us. The crops are good, and even the sickness doesn't seem to be as bad this year. I believe they will just question us or hold us for a time as a warning. When we are released we will have to spread the word that the proconsul is adopting a tougher policy and we may have to discontinue meetings altogether for some time."

"It is not likely that they will be able to hold you prisoner very long," Revocatus added, addressing his mistress, "because your father still has much influence, and as for your husband, well, nothing much can be done without the knowledge of the tribune Novius."

"That is true. Nothing much *is* done without his knowledge." The thought did not seem to give Perpetua much comfort. She turned sharply to the slave, "What did you mean by that?"

"Why, that, in spite of this secrecy, your husband will soon find you and obtain your release. What else could I mean?"

"But — " she hesitated, and then stopped altogether, not wanting to reveal to these others her greatest worry. How had they been discovered? Who had brought about their arrest? Her unfinished thought left a silence hanging over them all.

Saturninus spoke at last gently to Perpetua, for he could see that she was troubled by more than the natural fear of their fate that affected them all. "It is possible, mistress, that your husband was aware of this drive against Christians. He might even have authorized it under the direction of the governor — but he would have had no thought that it could become a threat to his own wife. He had no reason to connect you with the Christians. Did he?"

"I don't know. I don't know." Perpetua asked herself the same question but was unable to find the answer. She had never known until she talked to Tertullian over a year ago that her own mother and brother were Christians and had been she didn't know even now how long. Her father never dreamed of it, she knew. How often she had listened to his tirades comparing the Christians to termites or maggots spreading their evil slime in secret places and eating away at the pillars of the empire. And her mother and Mark showed nothing!

Novius was not nearly so bitter against the Christians, perhaps, she thought with a little disdain, because nothing seemed important to him except gratification of his appetites. Had he suspected that the change in her lately (and that had been apparent) was due to anything other than her recent motherhood? She had nowhere near the patience or the calmness of her mother, she knew.

But if it were to end in trial in the arena, they would see — he would see — how little she valued this body of hers. She closed her eyes and sat in the midst of the prisoners, rapt and far removed from their fears and terrors. She could hear the weeping of the girl beside her and she thought she should try to console her but she could not move or speak or open her eyes. She felt caught up and lifted and drawn away from the prison and from the prison of her own body.

High on a cloud above the earth she seemed to come to rest and looking down she could see hundreds of very small men swarming in among tiny buildings like the play blocks of her son. She could see the harbors with tiny boats in them and she could hear a busy hum coming up through the sky. While she watched the little figures hurrying below she saw one man come out of a doorway and look all around. Even though he was so small his face was clearly identifiable. She followed his figure in and out among the crowd, in and out among the buildings, until she saw him at last go to the harbor and get on one of the little boats. He was almost as big as the boat and as she watched he turned his face up and looked at her. Then he stretched out his hands toward her and he had something in his right hand, but she could not tell what it was. The sun glinted on it and it sparkled and gleamed bright and shining like a jewel — or a knife. Then he seemed to grow larger and larger, but still she could not distinguish what it was he had in his hand and she could not read the expression on his face. His hands reached farther and farther up into the sky, but just as it seemed as if they must touch her, a gust of wind lifted the cloud on which she rested and bore her out of reach and at last out of sight.

The silence in the room closed in about her, soft and protective like the cloud that had carried her, and she sank into a sleep that was clear and calm.

IV

FELICITY did not weep for very long, it made her breathing too painful. She forced herself to become quiet and take shallow regular breaths so that Revocatus would think her asleep, though he did not sleep she knew from the gentle pressure of his arm around her. She was surprised again that she could welcome the huge hairy arm about her, that she could be comforted by this surpassingly ugly and hardened slave whom she had been so reluctant to marry.

And yet, she thought, how can he comfort me? How can any of these know how it is with me? Three men, one old and near death in any event, and Perpetua — could anyone say she was not as strong as a man in spirit? Oh yes, she sighed for her baby, yet she seemed almost gone from the world already!

Among them Felicity was filled with life, vulnerable and sore in her whole body from the vigorous child she carried within her. Hardly had she sat down in an attitude of rest than the child began his most strenuous activity, adding to the turmoil already in her mind. If it should come to the ultimate choice, what could she do? Perhaps she could be a martyr for her faith — if it were very quick and there was not too much time to think about what was coming. But how could she expect this child to be a martyr, this child who had never heard of Christ? Was he to be catapulted straight into eternity without ever tasting life?

Again and again the tiny movements reminded her of the independent will of the child. Again and again the tiny fists and heels pummeled her as if they would compel her to bring them forth into this world.

Felicity tried to calm herself recalling the time two years before when she had first heard about Jesus Christ, at a moment in her awakening womanhood when she had been terrified to learn what the future might hold for her — a slave and a girl of unusual beauty, who had been brought up so kindly she hardly realized she was bound in servitude. Then it was comforting to hear about the love of a God who had become man, born of a woman, a woman no older than herself, grown to manhood, suffering abuse worse than any slave, and dying a frightful death for all mankind. His resurrection from the dead — here her mind could hardly follow. This it was that Perpetua saw, no doubt, but Felicity's mind and heart were fastened to the cross. Could she in no way leap over the agony to the glory beyond?

❋   ❋   ❋

Sleep would not come. Her mind wandered again under the pomegranates with the sound of the sea behind her. . . .

The day was soft and light. A fresh breeze from the ocean had brought an unusual late morning shower, so that the dark green leaves and orange-red blossoms of the pomegranate trees caught scraps and thimbles of rainbows from the sun overhead. Usually when the sun was high, the air was hard and bitter from the heat, but this day the sun was gentled by the clouds and the freshness on the ground felt like the morning dew.

Yet the land was silent. In the morning the birds, the small animals, the people would all be busy. Now the birds shook themselves on the branches, but they did not burst into song. The rabbits and ground squirrels stayed hidden in their burrows and under the leaves, untempted by the mock dawn. The people were all indoors and at rest, conditioned by habit to the inactivity of a semitropical midday.

At these times the sound of the sea obtruded, like the beat of the drums in an orchestra. The sea was the beat and pace and strength of life in Carthage, but its ceaseless voice was little heard.

Felicity, approaching through the rows of trees, was thankful for the sound of the surf now, though her bare feet made no noise on the wet grass. Her caution was evident in her pose, her body bent forward, her footsteps tiptoeing and hurried. Yet she was coming with a gay and breathless anticipation too, strangely and sweetly awakened because a handsome lad from the field had sought her out behind the kitchen and held her hand and spoken words of love. Only twice had he spoken with her because the occasions were few when field hands and household slaves could meet, so he had begged her to meet him during siesta time at a shed at the far end of the orchard where vegetables and fruits were stored temporarily until they could be sorted and brought to the kitchen or sent to market.

Here she was coming with a basket on her arm, for she intended to fill it with garden peas as an excuse for leaving the villa. As she drew closer to the shed her steps slowed, and she stooped in embarrassment to pick up a fragile scarlet petal on the ground. It always saddened her to see the blossoms fall, even though she knew the fruit must follow. Tomorrow this bright red petal would be brown and shriveled.

She could see no one about. Well, she thought, perhaps he was not able to slip away. At least she could collect the peas and perhaps sit a while shelling them.

She stepped into the darkness of the shed. Though it was roofed, it was without sides, yet so high on each side were piled baskets, some full, some empty in stacks, that scarcely any light came in, and she had to stay a minute to let her eyes adjust from the bright sunlight. The huge wicker basket with the fresh-picked peas was halfway down on the left side and there she hurried, for she did not like the dark narrow corridor and the silence.

She reached up to lift the peas out and drop them into her basket. The hamper was so tall she could not dip her basket in, but had to stand on tiptoe even to reach them with her fingers. Just at that moment two hands came around her and clasped her breasts, while a voice said close to her ear — "You have come, my sweet, my dearest — "

Felicity gasped, a little dismayed, not having thought to be surprised in that way. Then she gave a little laugh, and gently disengaged his hands. "You frightened me. I thought you weren't able to get away unnoticed. I must get the peas. They are my excuse." She turned aside from his eyes and held her empty basket helplessly, not wishing to raise her arms again.

Now it was his turn to laugh. He took the basket and in one movement filled it to the brim and set it in her hands again. He was tall, she thought, and how strong he looked in the dark. She had thought of him as just a lad. . . .

22

"Let us go out toward the sunlight," she suggested. "It is so gloomy in here. It quite depresses me."

"No, look, my sweet, here is a fine couch I have made for us where we can recline as any high-born Romans and eat all the fruits and tidbits we choose. Haven't you ever wanted to go to a lavish banquet?"

Indeed he had rugs (or rags, one could not see in the dim light) spread on the earth and a platter with grapes and figs and other fruits beside and he was very gay and attentive. She sat down gingerly, still holding the basket of peas. He flung himself down at full length with his head close to her and continued to ply her with fruit and light talk until she began to relax and enjoy the unusual dinner.

At last he handed her a pomegranate but she grew silent and would not take it, thinking of the girl Proserpina who had eaten the pomegranate seeds and had been forced to spend half her life with the god of the underworld. Suddenly she was frightened.

The man, misunderstanding her silence, agreed. "You are full, I know. . . . I didn't come to eat either. Now I think it's time you put down that wretched basket of peas — "

He tried to take it from her but she held on fiercely and jumped up, running in panic toward the sunlight at the end of the shed. Perhaps if he had had time, he could have won her, for her fear was not of the man himself but of the bluntness of the challenge to maturity. In time she might have laid aside her basket willingly. But time the man did not have, nor did he have the perception to understand her need. He was quite content with force. However, in his surprise, he was slower than the girl and did not catch up with her until she had reached the end of the corridor. She screamed when he seized her there but his hand cut off the

23

scream almost as soon as it had been uttered. The basket and the peas fell out of her hands as she struggled with him, but it was a very uneven struggle, and he lifted her easily and carried her back to the couch of rags.

He was careful to keep one hand over her mouth all the time, but he kept whispering to her, now in jest, now with threats. "At last we are rid of those peas, but keep silent, my love, do you want to be flogged until you are half dead? We must not be discovered — "

With threats and lovemaking he obtained from her a nodded assent that she would keep silence and removed his hand. Then she gasped and pleaded with him and wept (but quietly, for the threat of flogging had effectively gagged her). When these were to no avail, she struggled with all her strength (but still silently, from fear), and though the man could easily have overpowered her at once he did not, for the struggle was exceedingly pleasant and he preferred to prolong its delights rather than end it swiftly.

*　　*　　*

The slave did not know the young master was within hearing. No one in the household knew the many hours that Mark spent on the white cliff beyond the poplars overlooking the sea. Here at times the waves crashed against the very foot of the cliff, and at times the water rolled gently in and exposed as much as twenty feet of sand. The precipitous rocks rising thirty feet above the beach, broken and cut by the waves, had been a challenge to Mark in his boyhood. Now it was a retreat, to which he often came to study, to pray, or to restore himself with the sea and the sky.

In the stillness of the noontime the girl's sharp high scream was clear and startling in its abruptness above the low pounding of the surf. Yet in the stillness that followed, it took Mark some time to locate the place from which it had come. After he had looked about the orchard, the spilled basket of peas finally gave him the clue.

When he surprised the slave in the shed and saw who it was that he was trying to force his will upon, he was filled with a rage out of all proportion to the seriousness of the offense. For while slaves were not encouraged to indulge in idle pleasures and their masters preferred to stabilize their lives by regular marriages, still this was no crime.

But this was no ordinary slave! This was Felicity! She was just a child. . . . She was like his sister . . . his sister. . . .

He seized the man by his shoulder and threw him heavily to one side where he fell against a pile of baskets, spilling them out into the orchard row. Felicity shrank down on the rugs in terror. She had never seen the young master use violence on anyone before. The hardness and anger in his voice as he dismissed the slave frightened her. Now he turned toward her, and she was afraid all his wrath would fall on her.

But his voice changed and he spoke kindly, in his usual manner. "Are you all right?"

She nodded. "He said — we would be flogged — if I screamed — " She was so frightened she could hardly stammer out the words.

"He'll be flogged all right." Mark was curt. "But that's nothing for you to worry about. Come," he reached his hand to help her up, "I'll take you to my mother."

Felicity stood up, but when she was on her feet the world became black and whirling and she knew no more.

When Felicity regained consciousness she was lying on a pallet in the mistress' room and Claudia was sitting beside her on a cushion rubbing her wrists. With recollection her head began to spin again and a wave of nausea rose up in her that she could not control and, turning from her mistress, she vomited again and again. Then she was ashamed to see Claudia get a bowl and a rag to clean it up.

"No, no, please, let me," she begged. But Claudia pressed her down gently. "This was too much for you. Just rest."

Felicity could not reconcile this kindness with her stunning perception of her vulnerability and lack of freedom. How could one endure being at the mercy of anyone who came, any man with strength, any master with authority? Kindness or a flogging! What difference did it make? They were both dispensed without any will or power on her part. She was like a clam, forced by heat to expose its tender flesh, weak and totally without defenses. She did not trust the kindness and, in spite of her terror because of the slave's attack, she couldn't bear to think of him being flogged, because he had identified her with himself in slavery, and she felt that she must suffer even as he did.

"Will he be flogged?" she asked tremulously, and Claudia thought she wished reassurance as to the punishment. "He certainly will, and he will learn never to attempt such a thing again."

"Oh no, please," Felicity pleaded. "It was my fault, too. I went to meet him there, but I didn't know . . . I never thought . . ."

"He still should not have taken advantage of you. He deserves to be punished, and I've no doubt that Mark has already seen to it. I never saw him so angry. But from now on," she chided Felicity, "you had better think. . . ."

"What use is it to think when you are a slave?" The words flew out almost involuntarily, sprung from her helplessness. Claudia saw then that this shock had brought Felicity to a crisis where rest would not give her comfort nor kind words lift her from despair. Her youth and womanhood, crushed at the moment of awakening, cried for a restoration to wholeness and peace. She needed reality, not reassurance. But — how far was it safe to trust the child?

"Felicity, there is not one of us, whether master or slave, who does not suffer in this life. You think that we are fortunate and yet we were forced to flee in terror and poverty from Rome after Vivius had enjoyed great fortune and honor under the emperor, Marcus Aurelius. Commodus confiscated our property and would have had Vivius murdered because he spoke out against his corruption and vileness. We had to take passage for Carthage on a tiny ship that was so buffeted that both Mark and Perpetua were constantly ill. I knew nothing of it, for I was forced into labor prematurely and suffered terribly for three days before I gave birth to a stillborn son. They thought they would have to sew us both in the same sack, but I managed to cling to life for the sake of those two. Now we prosper, yet your master and I — "

Claudia stopped and sat still for a long time, debating whether to go on and how much to say. Then she continued, hesitating no longer.

"I don't know just how to tell you this. You have a need even as I had a need. We are all longing for some belief that will give meaning to life. Where can we find it?

"The Roman gods?" She spoke vehemently. "What use are they in sorrow or in suffering? They glorify youth and strength. They can give no answers to problems of death and sickness and old age.

"The men turn to philosophy. They would raise themselves beyond suffering, and by moderation and restraint become indifferent to the buffets of fate. But a woman knows she cannot be indifferent when she sees the child she has brought forth with such agony consigned to the sea. What we need is not less caring but more caring. Should we turn ourselves into heedless rocks? Philosophy has not the answer either.

"Only in the past year have I known what I missed and was longing for all my life. Mark returned from Athens a Christian and he told me about this religion which is so different from anything I had ever heard. How can I tell you so that you will understand? My heart recognized it as truth and accepted it with joy. But why? I don't know why except that I had a great sorrowful questioning, and here was the answer. You have a questioning too, but can I tell you the answer as I feel it?

"All people have the feeling that there is some power greater than themselves that controls the world and events over which they are powerless. Some call it Fate, some Chance, others the gods. But the Christians know that there is one God, and more than that, they know that God really loves each one of us, no matter how humble or weak or worthless we may seem to be. Because he cares, he sent his own son to teach us this truth and to teach us how to live. His own son — God himself — was born and lived and suffered and died even as we do. This truth is so wonderful it is almost impossible to believe, yet if we believe it, it clothes every aspect of our life with dignity. Surely if God himself was born of woman, birth is sanctified and womanhood made noble. If God himself suffered, was bound as a slave, tortured, stripped, and crucified, can we not accept the sufferings that we have as, in some way that we cannot understand, good and worthy?"

Felicity had listened silently, forgetting her despair in amazement at the revelation that her mistress was a Christian and in her wonder that she had told her this. But now, shocked by the one word, she exclaimed in disbelief, "How can you say that a man who was crucified is a god?"

"This man, Jesus Christ, died on the cross and was buried. But after three days he came forth from his tomb alive, and appeared to all his friends and remained with them forty days. Can a mere man do that? The grandfather of our priest, Saturus, heard it himself from a witness, John. John had been a good friend of Jesus Christ and had followed him for three years. Sorrowfully, yet still with hope, he watched him nailed to the cross. Then with numb despair he saw all his hopes shattered in the spear that pierced his master's heart and let out all his life's blood. In blank emptiness he helped wrap his stiff body and put it in the tomb. Yet three days later he saw that same Christ alive and well. Jesus, risen and glorified, ate with them and walked with them and brought them to an understanding of why he had to suffer and die, showed them a love so great that it hungered for man with an insatiable hunger to taste and share all of his life with him, his birth, his growth, his hope, his work, his suffering, his death, even his guilt. Love so great that suffering is absorbed and divinity extended. What can we not endure when God endures with us?

"Can you begin to feel a little the hope and truth of this? Somehow suffering is at the heart of the mystery, and the key to it is love."

❊   ❊   ❊

That first conversation had been two years ago, and several times after that, as often as Felicity was alone and not with Perpetua, Claudia talked with her and led her to a maturity and a deepening of spirit that was to help her in the events that followed.

Once Felicity asked Claudia why she did not speak to Perpetua about Christianity, and Claudia found it hard to answer. Her younger son, Gaius, was secretly taking instructions.

"It is so hard to decide when to speak and when to be silent. For it is not only ourselves we have to consider. Right now, Felicity, you hold all our lives in your hands. I am afraid that Perpetua would not accept Christianity at this time, and I would place this terrible burden on her for no purpose and at great risk to us all."

But as it happened Perpetua came to Christianity by a different road, and Felicity and Perpetua both began taking instructions from Saturus. It was at one of these meetings that they were apprehended.

V

About six miles from the city in the suburb of Megara was the home of Marcus Vivius Aelianus, the father of Perpetua. Aelianus had been proconsul in Carthage for one year under Marcus Aurelius and had purchased this large, rather remote acreage at that time. The older part of the house facing the road showed the straightened circumstances under which it had been built when he fled here with his family twenty years before. It was very small compared to the elaborate villas one passed on the way, of painted brick devoid of ornamentation, like the cottage of a farmer.

Though the exterior had been kept plain, the principal room in the original house was suitably transformed into a well-decorated formal atrium. Behind this, a large U had been added with spacious rooms built around a colonnaded courtyard which was open toward the sea. The court looked out upon a small formal garden protected on the north by a windbreak of tall poplars about twenty feet from the edge of a cliff overlooking the sea. To the west and south sloped terraces of vineyards, orchards, and gardens in neat and well-kept squares. It was a place of great natural beauty that had been developed by Aelianus with his own labor and planning.

Arriving in Carthage with only two slaves, one a city-bred Greek and the other his wife's personal slave, who became the mother of Felicity, he had taken a kind of Stoic joy in returning to the ancient Roman virtues and in tilling the earth and doing the planting with his own hands. Though he had many friends in Carthage, for he had been well liked as governor, he accepted nothing except their friendship when he returned as an exile. He took pride in the fact that it was his own vigor plus the natural fertility of the land that had brought him prosperity.

His well-earned success had indeed been substantial for he had added to his original holdings properties on the mainland. It was a long time since he himself had done any labor, but of late even the supervision had become too much for him, and he had relinquished to his oldest son almost the entire management of the estates. Though Mark had never worked in the fields as his father had, he often had accompanied the overseer Demetrius on his rounds, learning from him the skills that the Greek had discovered by hard experience. To Mark the cycle of growth and fruition was a never ending wonder, and it was in the love of the land that he came the closest to his father.

The same evening that the poor meal of gruel was given to the prisoners in Balbus' storeroom, Aelianus and his wife and sons were finishing their dinner, served as always in fair weather in the open courtyard of their home where all the activities of the family were centered. As was their custom Mark and Gaius and their father were reclining and conversing while Claudia sat and listened, only occasionally adding a word here and there. Aelianus had never been one to have separate meals for the men and women in his household. Even when he entertained, which was quite frequently, Claudia and Perpetua, before she was married, were honored guests. For one reason, he had great affection for his wife and great pride in his daughter, who spoke Greek as fluently as Latin and had a ready wit and keen intelligence, and, for another, he had observed it was the all-male gatherings that were the most apt to end in revelry and drunkenness of a kind abhorrent to his nature and philosophy.

Now as the fruit was brought in and the wine cups refilled, Aelianus brought up again the subject of Gaius' education, throwing out a question not as asking for advice, for he had made up his mind quite firmly, but by way of opening a discussion.

"What do you think, Mark, of Gaius' desire to study at Alexandria?"

"Frankly, I can't understand it," the older son replied. "Alexandria is all right. I've heard they have some good teachers, but I can't see why anyone would want to go to Alexandria if he could go to Athens. Athens is the very fountainhead of wisdom and learning. Just to walk in the agora where Socrates walked, challenging men to question themselves and their lives until all falseness and sham were stripped away — to follow where Plato carried this search to the kernel of goodness that is at the heart of man and of all existence — that is education."

"Yes, but you don't have to go to Athens to study Plato," Gaius retorted. "All of Greece is living on past glory. There is no Socrates there now, no Aristotle, not even a Zeno or Epicurus, just a lot of entombed philosophers and a handful of quick-talking mind-dazzlers cashing in on a reputation six hundred years old. Alexandria has life. It looks not to the past but to the future. To my mind it has the only group of original thinkers you will find."

"Originality doesn't mean truth," objected Aelianus. "Until you know what is best in the deposit of learning you cannot sift out the new to find out what is true and what is false. That is how errors like the Christian sect creep into our society, attracting not only the ignorant but even those supposedly well educated. There is something missing in the education to begin with, some flaw through which the falsehood seeps in, growing larger and larger until it swamps the intellect."

"But I have certainly had the fundamentals here, Father," Gaius protested. "You have planned every stage of my education and seen that I had the best teachers. I am so much more attracted to Alexandria than to Athens. Perhaps because I was born here in Africa, it seems that I could best find my place and expression at this school which is closer in space and in thought."

But this reasoning disturbed his father. "You're not African, Gaius, you're Roman. It's just that kind of talk that convinces me you are not to go to Alexandria. How can you take your place as a Roman citizen and, I hope, a Roman statesman, if you are bounded by a narrow provincialism?"

Gaius smiled — his was a bright spirit impossible to discourage or repress. "I can see that you are right, Father," he quickly conceded, so quickly that Mark suspected that this was the real purpose of the Alexandria buildup. "But I'm not Greek either. . . . What about Rome?"

The silence hung on the word, like an arrow on the target, sharp and hard and tremulous. Mark was amazed at his brother and at the same time envious. He would never have

34

dared to touch that sore spot in his father's memory, but then he did not have the directness of Gaius, nor his carelessness. Mark always studied everything he said. His friends in Athens had often mocked his deliberation. Never, as much as he admired quick repartee and clever answers, had he mastered them, for he was too careful not to give offense to anyone. Yet he knew, in spite of all his caution, or perhaps because of it, his father inclined more to the argumentative Perpetua and the impulsive Gaius. Now he watched his father who after the first shock of this frontal attack was preparing a reasoned reply.

"Ah, Rome — Rome! It is the place for a Vivius to be, yet I do not know how tenacious the memories are. Is it the place for a Vivius now?" He paused in reflection, then he resumed with decisiveness. "But for a surety, Rome is no place for a student. In five — ten — years' time with money, education, friends, and most of all, character, perhaps you could make your way at Rome. It is a dangerous life these days, trying to serve your country with honor, but it is important that some honorable men do so. Our emperor is a brilliant general and administrator, but there are many men needed to help rule all this empire. And the emperor is not always brilliant — " More he would not say of the licentious and depraved Commodus whose hatred had brought about Aelianus' own exile.

Mark tried to introduce a lighter note. "You'll like Athens, Gaius. The people are so friendly, interested in everything. They count the day lost they don't learn something new. They accept everyone and everything. You seldom see deliberate cruelty. Oh, not that the Athenians are without vices, but meanness and ugliness are not in them — "

Here Aelianus interposed. "Perhaps that is true, Mark, but

I count their universal tolerance as a point of weakness. Cruelty may sometimes be necessary to maintain power and the right. There are some things we ought not to tolerate — "

The sound of a horse's hoofbeats brought the conversation to an abrupt halt. Not many people came this far out without invitation and they were expecting no one. The horse was coming at a gallop but they heard it stop at their door. Gaius got up before the knock, curious to see whom the slave would be admitting, and hurried into the atrium. Claudia heard the exchange of greetings indicating it was Novius, their son-in-law. Then she heard loud cries of a child and she hurried into the atrium also.

She hardly noticed Novius, so shocked was she to see the bewildered and disheveled black woman holding Perpetua's child. The child was naked except for a blanket which had been wrapped about him, but on the wild ride his unswaddled legs and arms had kicked free. He looks like a savage, Claudia thought. How in the world can Perpetua allow that woman to care for her child?

"Where is Perpetua?" she asked in bewilderment at almost the exact time that Novius burst out with the same words.

"She is not here," she said, in reply to Novius, caught with sudden fear as she remembered where her daughter was to be that day. "Is she not at home?"

"Am I a fool to ride out here with this squalling child? I even had to lift the woman behind me on the horse after we passed the outskirts of the city or we wouldn't be here yet." Novius was livid with rage and indignation. A tribune wasn't used to riding with a black woman and a child. He was still in uniform. "I had just come off duty. . . . This slave tells me that Perpetua left an hour before midday. The boy is frantic with hunger. Where is she?" He shouted accusingly at them all, for Aelianus and Mark had also appeared.

Claudia said quietly to them, "Perpetua is missing." She spoke to Aelianus, but her eyes were on Mark, for he too knew where Perpetua was to be that day. She turned quickly to the slave, caught up the baby, and clasped him to her shoulder where the crying subsided to loud sucking noises as he pressed his mouth close to her soft flesh.

Aelianus turned to Novius. "What do you mean, Perpetua is missing?"

Novius explained again impatiently. "Just that. She left to go to the market with Felicity and Revocatus before noon and she is not back yet. I thought she must have come here. How could she leave the baby like that?"

"She did not even come home for dinner? But something must have happened to her. She would never leave the baby that long. Have you been to the authorities? . . . It is that slave Revocatus! Perpetua was always afraid of him! A fugitive — probably a murderer! How could you keep him around? He has taken this chance to escape again! Who knows what he has done to my daughter?" Aelianus was beside himself with agitation.

But Novius was equally vehement. "*Your* daughter has left her husband and abandoned her son — that is what has happened! I'd trust Revocatus with my own life!"

"Trust him with your life if you want, but did you have to trust him with two helpless girls?" Aelianus did not often raise his voice but now he shouted at his wife, "Will you get that baby out of here?" He wanted Claudia away as much as the child.

Hurriedly Claudia took the baby into her room at the back and sent one of the slaves out for a pitcher of goat's milk. Meanwhile she took a length of cloth and swaddled the squirming baby until his arms and legs were held tight to his body and only his lusty yells could any longer reveal his distress.

"There, my darling, my little one," she crooned. "You are a savage no longer. Soon you will have milk. Be still, be still. . . ." She held him again to her shoulder and walked back and forth until the slave came with the warm milk. Claudia first put a little milk in a spoon and put it in the child's mouth but it just dribbled out down his chin. Then she took a bit of honey and touched it to his tongue, and taking a small square of cloth she dipped it in the milk and put it to the boy's lips. He sucked on the cloth greedily, but it was a slow business, and each time she removed the cloth to saturate it again with milk he screamed his protests.

Claudia was so busy trying to satisfy the hungry baby that she did not notice that Gaius had entered until he spoke.

"They have left. Father and Novius and Mark all rode into the city. Do you know anything about this, Mother? Why would Perpetua leave the baby?"

"She would not leave him that long without food unless she were prevented from returning. I know that she was to go to Saturninus' today for instructions. All I can think is — they have been arrested."

"But wouldn't Novius know, Mother? He is simply wild. Seems to think she ran off and that's not the worst of it, she took his favorite slaves and left a most unwanted baby. I got the impression that if she had taken the baby and left Felicity and Revocatus, he wouldn't be searching so hard. Father is sure that Revocatus has kidnapped or murdered her — in broad daylight in the forum! If Mark weren't with them they'd be at each other's throats. But if she were arrested, Mother, wouldn't he know?"

"Who knows what he knows and doesn't know? I can't understand the man. I really used to like him. I never opposed their match, but I could see, after they were married, there was something. . . . I'm afraid now, Gaius, they must have been taken. What else could it be? If Minucius had not died, we would have some influence. But now I am worried. . . ."

"If Minucius were still proconsul, I doubt it would have happened. Hilarion is ambitious and wants to be noticed. No one likes him, but he doesn't mind that. He has his eyes only on the emperor and he means to make his impression. He might be reached with money, I don't know."

Claudia studied her son. The baby had fallen asleep in her arms, only partly full but exhausted by the hours of distress. "Gaius," she pleaded, "if it is as we fear, please, please, do as your father wishes and go to Athens. Mark has friends there, you will be safe, you can continue your instructions and be baptized. You heard Mark, everyone is accepted there. Please, Gaius, you must think of us — "

"I can't leave Perpetua, Mother. Could I let a girl suffer and not be at her side? What kind of a man do you think I am?"

But now Claudia was past reasoning or pleading. The exhaustion brought on by her fears and the struggling with the frantic baby unnerved her completely.

"Go, then, go! Disclose yourself to the authorities. Why should you worry about your mother or your father or this poor baby? If you go to Athens you can prepare a sanctuary for us, for this child, if need be — but why should you care? Go — Go — " And she fell to weeping and sobbing over the child with such violence that he awakened and started crying again. This simply increased his mother's sobbing and

Gaius, seeing she could not regain control in his presence, left to walk out into the courtyard. There the sound of the waves drew him and he walked to the bluff overlooking the sea and stood a long time watching the shifting black and silver of the night waters.

Finally he turned and walked slowly back to the house where everything was quiet. He went in to his mother who was again feeding the child with the slow unsatisfactory method she had improvised. He put his hands on her shoulders and kissed the top of her head. "I'm sorry, Mother. This is hard enough on you. I will do whatever you and Mark decide is right."

"I know how you feel, Gaius." Claudia was calm now. "If one of us could suffer in her place, we would offer ourselves in a minute. Why should a young mother die and an old woman like myself live? Ever since Mark returned from Athens a Christian, we two have been walking the edge of a chasm, into which one misstep would plunge us both — and others with us. A Christian cannot be passive and indifferent to others, yet each time we spoke to someone new we became more vulnerable. Can you remember the hunting down and execution of Christians six years ago? It was so close and terrible to my memory after I had become a Christian that I was frantic with fear at thoughts of torture and death. Now it seems to me that to step before the lions would be easier and nobler than to continue threading our way so meanly between duty and deceit, between our family and our faith.

"It is hard on Mark, too. He has never wanted anything else but to become a priest, yet he has forced himself to divide his time between clandestine study and the care of the estate just for my sake and your father's until you should come to manhood.

"What this will mean to us all we cannot know. We must simply have faith and pray, and then we can know the issue is of God and not of man and accept it in this way."

Claudia laid the sleeping baby down on a low bed of blankets in her room and covered him with a woolen cloth. Then taking a cloak for herself she went with Gaius into the courtyard where, with the sound of the sea before them and the soft blackness of the sky as a cover, silently and sleeplessly they watched the night through.

VI

I⊤ was not until the morning had half gone that Mark returned alone. Claudia had already fed the baby several times. All morning she had been holding the child, walking with him, rocking him in her arms, not so much because he was restless but because the restlessness was in her. Gaius had given in with the dawn and fallen asleep on the couch.

Mark's lips were in a thin line. His voice was hoarse and his breathing hard when he brought the news. "It is as we feared. Perpetua and four others have been seized as Christians. Get me wine and water. We got nothing from Novius. I must take money and go back at once. Felicity and Revocatus were with her. I don't know who the others are. Ah, at last."

Mark took the pitcher of water, poured some into the half-full goblet of wine and took a long draft. In haste he dashed some of the cold water on his wrists, and wetting a corner of his scarf wiped the dust and sweat from his face. The slave had also brought bread and cheese and he began to eat, telling his story hurriedly as he did so.

"It took so long to find out anything, because Novius refused to go to the pretorium. He didn't want to admit his wife had 'left' him, as he insisted. Father was just as certain she had been abducted or murdered by Revocatus, and that we should get the help of the authorities at once. Of course I could say nothing. There was nothing to do but wait until dawn when we could go to inquire down in the forum if anyone had seen her after she left the house.

"As luck would have it, Novius met a centurion he knew coming from the house of Balbus, the merchant who lives next to Saturninus, and he told him that Perpetua and four others had been arrested as Christians. But that was all he knew or all he would say. We didn't get to question him at all. He talked to Novius privately and hurried off.

"The forum was getting crowded so we couldn't talk there and we went back to Novius'. As soon as we entered father began to say something about its being preposterous to accuse Perpetua of being a Christian. And then Novius exploded.

"With much vile and abusive language he asserted that he knew she was a Christian and furthermore she had learned it in our house. He declared with an oath that she had never been a true wife to him and he intended to take legal steps for divorce. And then he said that he repudiated her child and forbade that he be called by his name! He finished by telling us (I won't repeat his words) to get out and never try to see or speak to him again.

"Father was so stunned by his accusations on top of the shock of hearing about Perpetua that he couldn't have remonstrated had he wanted to. I took him over to Crispus', cautioning him to say nothing about Perpetua for the time being. I think Crispus would still be his friend, but if even marriage and parental ties mean nothing, what can one expect of a friend?

"I think we might be able to get some information from

the centurion if I take money back with me. They are not being held in the prison. Father wants to see Perpetua and hear her deny the accusation. Of course we know she will never do that. But perhaps we could help them a little if we could find them and reach the right people. I hate to think of Felicity. . . ." He pushed away his cup hastily and rose.

Claudia called a slave to take the baby, and then took out her keys. "I'll get what money we have here, Mark. Later perhaps we might be able to get a loan on the harvest."

She hurried into Aelianus' office and soon came back with a heavy leathern bag. "There are ten sestercia here, Mark. While you are in the city, will you see about getting Gaius passage to Athens? If Novius suspects the whole family, there is no time to lose."

"I don't want to leave, Mark." Gaius was white and pleading, forgetful of his promise to his mother. "Please don't send me to Athens now. We must stay and suffer together."

"Ride with me, Gaius," Mark answered. "We'll talk on the way. First we must find out more. We'll be careful, Mother, and Gaius will ride back as soon as we learn anything. That way I can keep you informed and I won't have to leave Father."

"May God go with you!" Claudia kissed them and turned quickly away. She did not watch them as they rode off, but she could hear the hoofbeats of the horses growing fainter and fainter. The house was so still. The dread that had become dull and distant with familiarity confronted her now sharp and immediate in the empty house. Once she had thought it hard to lose a baby, but these — her sons, her daughter, in the full flower of maturity. Quietly she prayed, sorrowfully stricken by the demands of her faith, alternating

44

between the plea that her children be spared and a petition for strength if she must watch them go. How much easier it would be to suffer and die herself, if only she knew that they would live and be safe! But there was no safety — short of the final safety. If they were taken they would be the first to reach it — by a swift and dreadful route, it is true, but who could know the tortuous way and agonizing struggles ahead for those who were spared?

The crying of her daughter's son broke in upon the silence, and she rose quickly, with eagerness, to take up again the burden and the hope she had laid down for her brief farewell.

VII

Felicity had slept at last, and when she awakened she saw that daylight was lightening the open doorway. The men were standing and talking in low tones. Outside the doorway she could hear the heavy voices of the soldiers as the two men that had been left on night guard were relieved by four more.

One of the night guards laughed. "It won't take four of you to manage this lot. They're supposed to be Christians, and they never resist. Besides, there are two women and an old man among them. Not much fight there."

"Two women, eh?" one of the relieving soldiers echoed. "That should make this duty more interesting."

"You won't be interested in them, Lentulus," the night guard returned.

"Pretty ugly, eh? Old, too, I suppose."

"That's not what I meant."

"You're right. They're never too old or too ugly for Lentulus!"

One of the night guard retorted with a few words not in Latin, but in some patois familiar to the others, for it caused a great gust of laughter. The soldiers were of as varied nationalities as the prisoners, from every country except

46

Africa, since as a matter of policy native troops were never stationed in their homeland. Though they spoke Latin of necessity, among their own group their speech was an odd mixture, interspersed with many barbaric words and phrases, much of it unintelligible to anyone except another soldier, and specifically another soldier from the same legion. However, the prisoners could make out enough of the conversation to catch the meaning, and Revocatus could understand it all.

The night guard went off, and the four soldiers relaxed and began to unbuckle their armor. They had marched in in precise array, with helmets and breastplates glistening, but now they were looking forward to a day without interruption, so they were slouching about at ease. They had completely taken over the kitchen so that Balbus' slaves were forced to prepare his food in a small room at the back.

Two of the soldiers began playing at dice, and one prepared a bowl of cold grain and water for the prisoners. Lentulus was walking back and forth in front of the door to the storeroom trying to see the prisoners, but the contrast between the darkness inside and the morning sunlight in the kitchen was so great that he could do no more than make out the white tunics of the men, since they stood between the women and the doorway.

The soldier who was preparing breakfast for the prisoners glanced over at Lentulus.

"I knew a Christian once," he volunteered. "Do you remember old Harrobi, who ran "The Golden Apple" in Geisa?"

"Who could forget her?" Lentulus returned. "She had a face like a baboon and a disposition to match. Don't tell me she's a sample of Christians!"

47

"For a fact. She was telling me that after she died she would be young and beautiful and go around in white clothes, singing and laughing at us pagans burning in everlasting fire. Just for that, I told her, we won't let any of you Christians in the Elysian Fields either."

"The worms will have the last laugh at you both," Lentulus mocked. "But I thought Christians were supposed to love everybody. That old harridan! I can still hear her yell when some unlucky devil had a little more to drink than he had money enough to pay for."

"She really did love everybody, so she said, but people were always trying to take advantage of her. And that's why she kept those two Berbers. They weren't Christians, you see, and they'd just as soon stick a knife in your belly as eat. So that way she lost no money. She may have had dreams about a future life, but she held pretty tight to her stakes in this one."

"Well, I wish her good luck," Lentulus answered. "May she get her reward — and soon. As for me, I'd rather burn forever than spend an eternity in her company. But what have you there, Saetor? One bowl of gruel for five prisoners? How do you expect them to eat, like pigs? Here, let me fix up something, especially for our girls."

Lentulus quickly mixed more gruel from the sack of grain with which they were provided and taking both bowls he started for the doorway.

"I'll take this in for you, Saetor, so they'll know how kind and generous some soldiers can be."

"Watch it now, Lentulus," Saetor warned, for he knew his companion well. "You know the prisoners are strictly off limits." He used a Gallic word that had become accepted military slang.

"Oh, what's the matter with you, Saetor? You just got me interested. I'm curious to see if all Christians are like old Harrobi."

Lentulus entered the room and presented one of the bowls to Secundulus. "Move aside!" He pushed past Revocatus and Saturninus. "This is for the girls."

Perpetua took the bowl from the soldier quickly with a gracious "thank you," hoping this would remove his excuse for staying, but Lentulus made no move to go. He stood nonchalant and mocking, letting his eyes rove over the figures of the two women with a look that was as tangibly assaulting as a lecherous hand. Revocatus had stepped back to hold Felicity's hand, and he could feel her trembling and growing hot under the man's gaze until he felt on fire from her touch.

Finally when the silence had become as loud and tense as a scream, Lentulus cut into it with a mild query addressed to Perpetua in mock courtesy.

"I am very interested in Christians, mistress. Can you tell me a little about what you believe? I've been told that you love everyone, even your enemies — or your captors. But that hardly seems possible. Is that really true?"

"Yes, it is true," Perpetua replied, holding her voice and her eyes steady. She was almost as tall as he was, and she met his look directly. If she had fear, it was not apparent.

Lentulus grinned for this was the answer he wanted. These girls were a far cry from old Harrobi. "What a strange and interesting idea! I'm all in favor of love myself. But I'd like to hear you say it from your own lovely lips. Do you really love me?"

"Yes, I love you," Perpetua replied without hesitation, though the contempt in her eyes gave the lie to her words.

"I love you, even as our Lord loved the most depraved sinners, the most grotesque madmen, the most loathsome of lepers. I love you with pity and sorrow to see the man you could be and the beast you would become."

Perpetua was well practiced in the use of words, and Lentulus, awed by her fearlessness and her patrician superiority, could not find a ready answer. He turned instead to Felicity. The little slave girl offered more sport, he decided, and she was prettier besides.

"Well, how about you, my dear?" He spoke condescendingly to her as fitting her position. "Do you also love your enemies? It is quite evident that you love indeed." An interesting idea now came to him. "Is your husband here — if you have a husband?" But she was still silent, only pressing her hand tight in Revocatus', so that he exclaimed, "Not this ugly wretch surely! For a beautiful girl like you! This is really a mockery! I can well believe that in the darkness of one of your Christian love feasts you took a likelier fellow as father for your child — "

He paused, highly amused at the fury apparent in the tense body of Revocatus.

"And you, scum that you are," he taunted him. "You are a true Christian. You love me, don't you, even if I should beat you or kill you?" He pushed a big hand in Revocatus' face and shoved him contemptuously back against the wall. "You love me still, don't you!" His eyes were still on Revocatus. "Even if I ravish your wife before your eyes — " He turned suddenly and seized Felicity, but he had so sooner touched her when he felt his throat gripped in a vise of iron. His hands flew up in defense, but the grasp of the slave's fingers was impossible for him to break, and the pressure increased remorselessly on the taut muscles of his neck.

Saetor, who had been watching from the doorway, shouted to the other soldiers and himself jumped in behind the slave to pull him from Lentulus. But such was Revocatus' fury and strength that it took all three men to subdue him and pinion his arms. By this time Lentulus was gasping and the marks on his throat were deep and red. He looked at Revocatus still struggling in the soldiers' hands. Then with a quick movement he unbuckled his sword and raising it, still sheathed, smashed the hilt with all his force into the face of the slave. Revocatus, seeing the blow coming, flung back his head to catch the full force of the blow on his mouth and jaw.

Saetor let go of Revocatus and shouted at Lentulus, "You're a fool, Lentulus! What will the centurion say when he sees this? We'll all be in trouble because of you!"

Lentulus gave a short laugh. "One more mark on that ugly face doesn't even show. Who would notice, much less care?"

Then he turned his back and sauntered out, oblivious alike to the hatred of the prisoner and the scorn of his fellow soldiers. Saetor and the others talked in low tones, after which they drew lots, and one took a position as guard athwart the entrance to the prisoners' room.

Lentulus derided, "Christians, bah! They say one thing and mean another. Why do the authorities bother with incense and sacrifice? That doesn't prove a thing. I could tell in a minute whether a person is really a Christian or not. The only trouble is, if they used my test, there'd be nobody left to feed the lions."

The man at the door took him down a peg. "If you have to have three men to back you up, you'd better think twice about these tests or you'll never live long enough to try another one."

51

Revocatus spat in the direction of the doorway. His mouth was full of blood, his upper lip was cut and a long gash continued in a curve from his lower lip to the back of his jaw. Felicity's stomach churned to see the blood and teeth that came from his mouth as he spat. Blood was dripping unheeded onto his chest and the wound on his face gaped like a misplaced mouth, horrible and askew and grinning. The sight made her sick and dizzy but, struggling against her own weakness, she came close to him and pressed her folded veil against the wound to stop the flow of blood and to hide the raw flesh.

Revocatus was still standing tense and charged with fury, until her touch recalled him from his madness. He raised his hand to cup the veil on his jaw, removed her hand, and drew her to his other side.

"It is nothing," he said, looking down at her with the utmost tenderness and gentleness. "It is nothing." And it was as nothing to him, for the action and the violence had elated him as his manhood demanded after being hedged and hemmed in by shadows. The pain in his mouth and jaw set his nerves tingling and gave him a perverse kind of pleasure. He still savored the feel of the man's throat beneath his hands, glorying in the defeat that he had administered to four armed soldiers. For wasn't she safe and the soldiers gone?

"The fellow is right, Felicity. I am no Christian." Painful as it was to speak, he had to tell her what was in his heart. He held her close and whispered, "I want only to be with you. If you live, I live. If you die, I die." He stroked her hair. "What made you love me? What made you come to me that first night so willingly? One minute of your love is worth more than my whole life before. This I can die for, willingly and with my whole heart. But I don't think that makes me a Christian."

"Who is a Christian?" Saturninus put in, hoping to quiet the feelings of horror with which they were all filled and having heard only the first words spoken by Revocatus. "We are becoming Christians each day, but even when we are baptized does that guarantee we will always be Christians in our hearts from that time on? I sit with my pots all day, and I have such a longing for the little clay gods and goddesses I used to make. To mold the mud and clay of the earth into the semblance of living flesh — I almost felt a god myself. It is such an insignificant thing to trouble about, yet to give up my life doesn't go much more against my nature, and that has to be done only once."

"Only once, it is true," echoed Secundulus. "And the issue is clear cut, so that it is easy to know what is right and what is wrong. How often is the answer that clear? We decide today and the next day we meet the same problem in a different shape and find to our dismay that we were completely and righteously in error. But there is no doubt about this decision, and there is no doubt about our reward if we persevere. This way we put an end to the conflict once and for all. Perhaps it is easier to die as a Christian than to live as one."

Felicity said nothing but pressed close to Revocatus answering his secret words with the pressure of her body. She put her fingers to her lips and gently touched his wounded and swollen mouth. To her that wound was a prideful thing, a mark of love, a beautiful disfigurement. They can talk about how easy it is to die, these old men, she thought, but here in this gloomy prison she was loved and protected — and she was not ready to die at all.

53

VIII

REVOCATUS held Felicity and the pressure of her body on his stirred in him not so much a hunger as an overwhelming tenderness, all the greater since he had not known he had such emotion within himself. It seemed almost as if Felicity had given it to him and he was now giving it back to her.

Of himself he had nothing but violence. Seized for a slave in the hills of Thrace while still a youth, he had passed from one master to another, valued for his strength, yet constantly abused in an attempt to make him conform to his master's will. His back was crisscrossed with scars from the lash and his face marked by many blows. His strength and violent temper had made him feared and hated by his fellow slaves, who took every opportunity to inform on him with the result that his escape had been doomed to failure from the start.

After his recapture no one would have him except the stone merchants, who took only the most incorrigible slaves and hardened criminals to work in the limestone quarries that supplied most of the building material for Carthage. These quarries were worked entirely from the sea; there was no land entrance. The slaves were brought in by boat and, once there, never left the caves. Supplies were brought in and rocks removed by boat. Occasionally one of the criminals with a three-year sentence or less would survive the heavy work and the limestone dust to be released at the end of his term, but the only release a slave could expect was death, and even that did not take him far. One of the limestone rocks he had quarried was set aside to accompany his body to the depths of the sea. The very mention of the quarries was enough to make the most recalcitrant slave docile.

It was in the string of slaves destined for the quarry that Novius noticed Revocatus. They were all chained together, but he was confined also by manacles and leg irons. His size and strength made him conspicuous among the others and his unsubdued rebelliousness still showed in his bearing in spite of the branding and the marks of the lash and the double fetters. Prompted by impulse Novius bought him and took him back to Geisa as his personal attendant. Perhaps Revocatus was grateful for having been snatched from living death or perhaps he responded to a kind of respect that Novius gave him as man to man. There was the same kind of wild pride in them both that recognized its distorted image even as a man who sees a bulbous, squatty face in a globe or a flaccid shape in disturbed waters knows himself though he laughs and does not count it a true picture. In the two years that Revocatus was with Novius in Numidia, he served his new master for the first time with an ungrudging loyalty, and on more than one occasion Novius felt that he owed his life to the impulse that had brought him such a formidable ally.

The last sortie in which Novius took part was an instance. Having received word that a band of raiders was attacking a village, Novius led out a troop to drive them off. In the fighting outside the village he took an arrow in the groin and fell from his horse. The tribesmen, pursued by the troops, made a large circle and doubled back on their tracks. Revocatus had stayed behind to construct a litter so that the men of the village could carry his master back to the base, since the wound made it impossible for him to ride. Suddenly the Numidians came in sight again and at their shouts the villagers scattered. Revocatus concealed Novius behind a clump of bushes, and mounting his horse, with shouts and taunts, drew the barbarians after him.

The ruse was successful and when the Roman troops returned, Novius was able to attract their attention and get help. For twenty days nothing was heard or seen of Revocatus, and Novius was certain he had succumbed either to the spears of the Numidians or to the lure of freedom. But he did return at last, with nothing to say about the twenty days that he had been missing, and since that time there was a greater understanding and comradeship between master and man, and Novius allowed Revocatus a large degree of freedom and trust.

This sortie was the end of Novius' active campaigning for the time being. He returned to Carthage with Revocatus for lighter duty. It was then that he met Perpetua through Fiducius Minucius, the proconsul, who was a friend of her father.

After their marriage, Perpetua asked Novius to sell Revocatus because she did not trust him and could hardly bear to have him around, but Novius made light of her request at first.

"Revocatus is like an old shoe. He suits me perfectly and no one else would give a plugged denarius for him."

"The master of the gladiators would pay a good price for

him, I'm sure," Perpetua answered quickly. "He's absolutely no use as a house slave. He can't get along with the others, and there's really nothing for him to do except carry the food home from market."

"Well, I hope we won't be in Carthage forever," Novius remarked. "And he will be useful to me in the future."

"I really think he'd like being a gladiator," Perpetua persisted. "This idleness is not good for him."

But Novius impatiently put an end to the discussion. "I'm not sending Revocatus into the arena," he stated unequivocably. "So let us hear no more about it."

Revocatus well knew the revulsion with which his master's wife regarded him, for she never troubled to disguise her dislike and fear. He had no reason to believe that her feelings were not shared by Felicity. The girl had always spoken to him pleasantly, it is true, but she avoided him as much as possible, and when she did look at him her eyes had the wary frightened look of a gazelle suddenly scenting a lion.

When Novius told Revocatus that he intended to marry Felicity to him, Revocatus simply laughed, not considering it seriously at all. Perpetua was right; he was not a good house slave, nor did he even enjoy it. He was uneasy and confused in this quiet domestic life at Carthage. Unused as he was to the more humane side of servitude, he was suspicious of the customs with which he was unfamiliar. Marriage among slaves had no reality to him; it was a specious appearance of freedom where freedom did not exist. Besides, he was only too well aware of the sardonic humor of his master. Three years ago it had been a torment to him, and he had had to fight himself fiercely, remembering the quarries, to keep from flying into a rage when mocked.

Gradually he learned to accept Novius' jests and mockery as just his way and to pass them off with a laugh or rough jest in return. So he laughed now, but he felt tensed inside, bracing himself against some threat he could not visualize.

As the time for the "marriage" came closer and the tension between his master and mistress mounted, he began to believe that, whatever the joke was, it was not on him. The situation still made him uneasy, but, he reflected, why should he worry since it was possible that he might even gain some temporary pleasure from this dubious prospect.

The marriage ceremony was a simple and brief exchange of vows in the presence of their master and mistress. When Felicity said the formula, "Where you are Gaius, I am Gaia," her voice shook and her hand was like ice when she put it in his. She looked serious and thoughtful, not as if she were acting a part. But to Revocatus the words sounded strange and alien, for they were not a part of the life he knew, but seemed a grotesque mummery of Roman things, like the comic mimicry of a monkey. He resented being made to appear a monkey or a parrot mouthing words without meaning, and he felt he was being obliged to perform for the amusement of his master.

When he was able to take Felicity to the room that they had been given, he was still touched with anger at the travesty, as he felt it, in which he had taken part. He seized her then, for force was all he had knowledge of, and there was more of resentment than passion in his grasp, but when she yielded without resistance and he felt her softness close to him, he was made keenly aware of her trembling and the furious beating of her heart. She has been forced, too, he thought; they were both victims, pawns in this game Novius was playing. Looking down suddenly, he surprised a flash of fright in the girl's eyes, and it gave him a momentary insight. Whatever his purpose, he suspected that his master had cast him in the role of villain and that he was playing his part only too well.

"You are afraid of me," he said, trying to look into her eyes again. But she was silent and kept her eyes down. He felt a sudden shame and released her. Mockery or not, she had come to him as his wife, not an evening's purchased pleasure or a piece of booty to be enjoyed and discarded.

"I have hurt you," he said with remorse, wanting to atone for his roughness. "I'm sorry. I didn't mean to hurt you. Please believe me. Please don't be afraid of me." His voice was quiet and pleading.

She looked up then and pressed her hands hard against her upper arms trying to still her trembling. She looked into his eyes for a long time and at last she grew calm and was able to speak with steadiness. "I am not going to be afraid of you any more." She spoke with a quiet determination and then smiled in an open and generous acceptance of his apology.

He looked at her clearly now that the cloud of resentment had lifted, and he was overwhelmed by her loveliness and kindness in comparison with his own coarseness. Now he thought not so much that he must possess her but that he must make sure that never, never would she have any cause to regret coming to him. He felt humble and awkward before her, and he did not know how to express his thoughts.

"Can you bear to live as my wife, seeing what kind of man I am?"

"I do not know what kind of man you are," she answered gently.

"You are so beautiful and I — "

59

But she interrupted almost angrily. "Is beauty all you think of?" Her anger and her words were not directed toward him but spilled over from the memory of those others who had desired to possess not her love but her beauty only. "How I wish I were not beautiful! Perhaps then some time I might be loved for myself alone."

Her words were intense and there was no fright or revulsion in her eyes, but only sincerity. Her wish to be loved entered his soul and gave form for the first time to the unconscious pressure within him which he had never thought could even be put into a wish, much less be sought after. He was challenged by hope yet unable to believe that he could really meet this lovely creature and with her seek out not only the fulfillment of desire but the quieting of the whole soul's yearning. Yet she was asking him — asking him to love her. He wanted to satisfy her, he wanted so much to love her, but he was heavily conscious of his own inadequacy.

"I am not fit to touch you," he said in a low voice. "I do not know how to love."

She reached out then and took his hand in hers in a gesture at once shy and bold. She drew near to him and her head was close to his breast and her hair sweet and soft beneath his lips, and he could no longer keep from enfolding her in the circle of his arms. After a long time, gently and gratefully they came together, and in them both was a great quiet wonder.

IX

AFTER Mark had left Aelianus at Crispus' house, the old man was hard put to answer his host with any degree of coherence. Mark had explained that business of a serious nature had compelled his father to be up all night and he asked refreshment for him until he, Mark, could return. Aelianus would take nothing to eat or drink, however, but pleaded fatigue and begged for a couch and a quiet room.

When this was furnished, his weariness made him recline but his thoughts gave him no rest. His worries were less about Perpetua than before, since he had envisioned her murdered or ravished. The arrest was not serious, for a charge of this nature could be dismissed by a simple denial by the accused and an offering to the gods. What was incomprehensible to him was the accusation of Novius that she had learned Christianity at his house. His own views on Christianity were surely well known to everyone. Hadn't he been a trusted aide of Marcus Aurelius and concurred with him completely in his measures for the suppression of this seditious group?

Unless Novius could have been referring to Tertullian. Yet it was four years since Tertullian entered his house. In the past the lawyer had been a frequent visitor since they had a common interest in law and philosophy and, though Carthage was large, the circle of truly educated Romans was small. But after he had championed the Christians in his writings Aelianus had never seen or spoken to him again.

It was after the execution of a number of Christians by the proconsul Remigius that Tertullian had spoken out so vigorously in their behalf. Aelianus could at first understand their defense by Tertullian because Remigius had prosecuted the matter with outrageous appeals to emotion, and anyone with any legal training could find innumerable inconsistencies in the charges.

It made a mockery of the law to say that persons were deserving of death because of imputed and unproven crimes, and it disgusted a man of reason to see someone who was charged with cannibalism released on a promise to quit the "error." The ill-advised policy of the proconsul had provoked Tertullian into refuting these specious charges, but apparently in so doing he had convinced himself that the Christians were completely in the right. It was strange to see how that brilliant intellect could have become so clouded.

Apparently Hilarion was using the same ill-considered tactics in a clumsy play for power. To bring Felicity to public trial, whether she were freed or not, would simply enlist the sympathy even of the mob on behalf of Christians. The punishment of Revocatus the crowd would relish, no doubt, but much as Aelianus disliked the slave, he could see there was no justice in accusing him. For basically the crime of Christianity was treason. The morals of the individual mattered not at all, it was a question of where one's allegiance lay. In this light it was absurd to take action against a child or a slave. Let the slaves have their faith

62

if they wished — it harmed no one. A citizen or a free man who benefited from the state was bound to loyalty. Let such a man, if accused of Christianity, be tried with reason and dignity appropriate to his status and executed if guilty in a suitable manner. These slave hunts and wild-beast shows were more suited to barbarians than to Romans.

But Perpetua? How could this smear have become attached to her? Some vicious person had invented a lie, no doubt. But it was surprising that Novius had swallowed it completely. He had always thought the man had good judgment. Of course he was very ambitious — it was one of the qualities he admired in his son-in-law — perhaps the fear of scandal had touched off his outburst this morning. He was overwrought, beyond a doubt, and surely once Perpetua had been completely cleared of this charge, the matter could be put at rest. That nonsense about repudiating his son!

So Aelianus tried to quiet his worries, yet he could not forget the charges Novius had made, nor the bitter manner and virulent words in which they were uttered.

    ❋   ❋   ❋

When Mark returned a little after noon — for he had pressed his horse hard both ways — he had not only the money but the information as to where the prisoners were being held. This he did not reveal in front of Crispus, but he induced Aelianus to take a little wine and water, and when they were on the street, he told his father that the five prisoners were being held at the very house in front of which the centurion had accosted Novius that morning.

"I went to the forum first when I returned, thinking someone else might have seen something, and did in fact discover that a potter named Saturninus and his father had

also been arrested. His wife saw the soldiers take the prisoners next door. Gaius came back with me and he is waiting
at the shop of Saturninus now."

Mark had of course known very well where to make in-
quiries, but even so he had been surprised at the ease with
which he discovered the location of the prisoners. They
spoke no more on the street, for fear of being overheard,
but they were soon at the potter's shop. A bell tinkled as
they opened the door, and Gaius, who had been idly gazing
at the rows of pots, came over to greet them at once. Irene,
the wife of Saturninus, had come from a back room at the
sound of the bell and waited for the exchange of greetings
before coming forward. She was a fat, shapeless woman, her
hair perpetually in disarray, on whom even the simplest
garment looked untidy. She was completely oblivious of her
appearance, and, after she smiled, so was everyone else, so
warmed were they by her friendliness.

Now as she came forward with the warm and pleasant
smile lighting her face, Mark spoke quickly as if to a stranger, fearing she might reveal something before his father.
He need not have worried, however, for Irene was well used
to caution, since she had been a Christian even before the
last persecution and had managed to escape detection. Her
smile now was the same as for any customer, and with a
noncommittal greeting she took them to a back room with
a rear entrance opposite that in Balbus' house. Mark gave
her a coin at his father's bidding and a warm handclasp
behind his father's back and they were left alone.

"I have ten sestercia, Father," Mark said, bringing out the
leathern bag. "It was all we had on hand."

"Oh, I doubt if we'll need it at all now, Mark." Aelianus
was cheerful and resolute now that the first hurdle had been

64

overcome so quickly. "It was very resourceful of you to find out the location of the prison. But I'm sure now that if I present myself to the centurion in charge here I will be able to speak to my daughter without delay. Once I hear the denial from her lips, I can go straight to the proconsul and demand a hearing. There is no need for bribery and no excuse for it when there is no guilt."

"Nevertheless, Father, take the money, in the event you find it difficult to see Perpetua. Or will you let me go and see what I can find out first?" Mark wished he might postpone the moment when father and daughter met — if only he could see her first instead — but then his father must learn some time.

"I will go next door at once." Aelianus rejected Mark's offer. "Were they taken in the back? The woman's husband was arrested too, you say?"

"Husband and father-in-law. They run the shop here. She is a midwife and well respected hereabouts."

"Do you suppose she is a Christian, too? Must be, if her husband is. She seems a pleasant woman, but you can't tell from appearances. Be of good cheer, sons. I hope you will soon have good news to take to your mother!"

Mark handed the bag of money to his father, but he could not meet his eyes nor find words to answer. He watched his father cross to the back of the adjoining house. His step was strong, his back straight and youthful, even though his hair was white. How would he react to the shock that was in store for him? Perpetua had always been his favorite — she was so much like him in many ways. That was one of the reasons his mother had not tried to interest Perpetua in Christianity. "I'm afraid," she had said, "it could mean the destruction of us all."

Caution! Caution! Where did caution stop and cowardice begin? For he was guilty, too. Of caution? Of carefulness? Of cowardice?

"He has been admitted," Gaius said, for he was now standing beside Mark watching. His eyes were bright. "And when he returns, shall we not also declare ourselves and prepare to die at our sister's side?"

"No," Mark said. How simple everything was for Gaius! Nothing was ever that simple for him. Even now he could see, on the one hand, Gaius' readiness and eagerness and, on the other hand, his lack of knowledge, his unseasoned faith. Did he really want to die for love of God or love of glory? And how about himself? Was he considering his mother and father now, or was he being a coward in urging caution?

"No," he repeated, and this time he was answering his own question. This time he was right. He could not strike his father deliberately and wound his mother so with his own hands.

"No, Gaius, there is no reason for us to go out of our way to get into trouble. Do you want to leave your mother totally alone? She needs us with her as long as we can stay. She must face the same threat. This is the time for caution, not boldness. But I see no need for you to flee to Athens either. Mother is oversolicitous. We may be able to help Perpetua if we stay. If it is God's will that we be taken, we shall at least be together."

And with this understanding Gaius was content to wait.

X

PERPETUA had kept aloof from the other prisoners in the afternoon. The centurion had come in about noon and whether he had noticed anything or had stricter orders concerning the guard, he remained the rest of the day and the soldiers were disciplined and orderly. He had even had a bowl of soup taken in to Felicity, and the noon meal passed without incident. Since Revocatus could hardly move his lips Felicity gave him the soup that had been brought in for her. She had torn two pieces from the cleanest part of her veil and made a rough bandage which she tied about his head to hold the gaping wound closed.

Whether it was the food or the orderly attitude of the soldiers, the prisoners seemed to relax and were quite cheerful, laughing as Saturninus told stories about his shop and Secundulus recalled amusing incidents about a parrot which he had trained to talk. The bird used to sit on a shelf near the door of the shop and scream in raucous imitation of the human voice, "What cha going to buy? What cha going to buy?"

"The customers always got a laugh out of him," Saturninus recalled. "Maybe business would still be good if the bird hadn't died."

Perpetua privately thought they would have been doing better to spend their time in prayer, but she had the good sense to realize that she herself was irritable because of her discomfort and no fit adviser. However, the open affection of Revocatus and Felicity made her impatient, and the admission of Saturninus that he still longed to create statues of gods and goddesses was to her completely incomprehensible.

To be a Christian had to Perpetua been a total dedication. Subordination of the desires of the flesh to those of the spirit was not a constant struggle but a single joyful renunciation. To her the talk of becoming a Christian each day was nonsense.

Perpetua's attraction to Christianity had come about rather strangely soon after she was married and, to understand it, it is necessary to go back to the day that Perpetua first met Novius.

The young tribune had been invited to dinner at the Villa Vivia with Fiducius Minucius, the proconsul, and two other officials and their wives. Perpetua knew them all well with the exception of the recuperating officer, for they often entertained and were entertained in mixed groups. Through the entire dinner hour Novius regaled the others with stories of his adventures during his four years' campaign in Numidia. He seemed a veritable modern Ulysses in the charm of his story-telling and, she suspected, in the veracity of the tales. The other ladies were quite agog, hanging upon his words and exclaiming over his bravery. A fool, Perpetua thought, a witless fool, covering up by braggadocio what he lacks in intelligence.

"Tell me, sir," she broke in, "what attracts a man to the life of a soldier? Sometimes I wonder if a soldier's apparent bravery does not spring from a fear of failure in the normal pursuits of life."

Her father, as host, was a little distressed by this thinly disguised attack, but Novius readily accepted the challenge.

"You're right, mistress," he answered, "it is fear that made me a soldier. But it is not the fear of failure in these 'normal pursuits' as you call them, it is the fear of being stifled, of being bored, of dying through inertia. Give me a worthy opponent in the forum and I'll duel him as readily with words as I fight the barbarians with the sword. Death is not important. The danger adds a little zest, but it does not really matter. What really counts is the *agon,* the contest, and the outcome doesn't matter either, win or lose, it is the *agon* that counts."

"But is not all of our life an *agon?*"

"Oh no, not so. Not in Carthage at least. Here those inferior in station kowtow to their superiors, and our peers can find nothing better to compete about except the virtue, or lack of it, of their current heart interest. The only contest you ever find is a noble bout with a street vendor, haggling over the price of a duck."

"You seek the *agon* in externals only, sir. Look within. The greatest adversary is in ourselves, and the greatest victory is one we can achieve through self-mastery."

"You have shown me another, mistress," Novius answered with a smile, for he was intrigued by Perpetua's directness and lack of coquetry in contrast to the cloying adulation of the other Carthaginian women he had met. "You have shown me a worthy opponent with whom I am ready to match wits at any time."

Such became the pattern of Novius' courtship of Perpetua, a constant intellectual battle with no false deference to sex. Every encounter between them was stimulating, every meeting a challenge. Perpetua found that Novius was by no means a fool, and she began to see in him a younger reflection of her father, philosophical, ambitious, dedicated to the Stoic principles of pursuit of truth and service to his country.

In her background — her closeness to her father, her education equivalent to that of her brothers, her association with her father's circle of friends on terms of intellectual equality, and even the odd nature of Novius' courtship that paid tribute to her mind rather than her womanhood — nothing in this background had prepared her for the passionate surrender her husband expected in marriage. Having entered into marriage with pride, she felt used and degraded in the physical relationship, and the more ardor and passion Novius showed in an attempt to break down her reserve, the more she recoiled.

Perhaps if Novius had been home more she might have been able to recapture the intellectual rapport that had existed between them before their marriage, but at this time she scarcely ever saw him except at night. The proconsul was ill, and Hilarion, who had been appointed temporarily to take over his duties, relied a great deal upon his senior officer. Novius had been in Africa for five years as military tribune, four years on active campaign in Numidia, and this past year in Carthage. It was an easier, less dangerous life in Carthage, but he did not allow it to be easy. Work and learn was his formula and he never spared himself. He had his eyes on the office of imperial legate in charge of the whole legion in Numidia, a position no less important than that of proconsul and in contrast a long-term appointment by the emperor himself. It was a life that appealed more to Novius than this sedentary one at Carthage. There was an established base at Geisa, and both officers and men were able to have their families with them, but it was still a rugged frontier existence full of action and violence. Novius hungered for a return to it, for his spirit was restless and greedy, if inconstant, longing to sample every sensation, every feeling, every thought. His body demanded excitement in the same way that his mind craved stimulation.

Now he saw an opportunity to fulfill his ambition by making himself indispensable to the man who was to be the next proconsul, and he threw himself into his work with all his skill and energy with the result that Perpetua felt completely ignored and shut out of every part of his life — except one.

In an attempt to work out the conflict between what seemed to her Novius' excessive demands and her own instinctive repulsion, she turned characteristically to philosophy. She remembered the vigorous discussions at her father's house and especially the brilliance of the lawyer Tertullian, his acid paradoxes and the depth of his perception. With a half-guilty curiosity she turned to his writings now. In his advice to married women she found sentiments with which she felt heartily in accord.

His castigation of the wiles and devices used by married women to beguile their husbands and his praise of modesty and chastity in wives she read as condemnation of overindulgence and even overenjoyment of marital pleasures. It confirmed her in her belief that a wife need only to conduct herself with virtue and purity and to give to her husband obedience and submission.

Yet, as she read on, she found she could not accept these

thoughts without pursuing further into the causes and motives of human action. She felt that her life as it was had neither purpose nor stability. For if she based her actions on her desires or on those of her husband, she was no different from the sands of the desert shifting with every wind. Some standard she was seeking, some aim, some guide that was true and unchanging.

Then she came to Tertullian's challenge —

"The very obstinacy of Christians in the face of torture and death is the teacher. For who is not stirred by the contemplation of it to inquire what is really beneath the surface? And who, when he has inquired, does not become one of us? And who, when he has become one of us, does not desire to suffer also?"

Dared she inquire? Dared she, if she were really seeking the truth, refuse to inquire?

It was then that she sought Tertullian out. She saw him only once, but at that time they talked for three hours, and she came away convinced that only in the love of God and the love of Christ would she find completion. Only one thing bothered her and that was the revelation by Tertullian that her mother and brother were Christians. She couldn't understand why they had failed to share their faith with her, and when she saw her mother, she made this disappointment plain.

"Now I can see I was wrong," Claudia admitted, "but at the time I did what I thought was best for us all. Put yourself in my place. Can you imagine trying to convert your father? I thought you were so close to him that there was little likelihood you would be receptive at all. Besides, you were promised to Novius, and I know myself how hard it

72

is to maintain a proper and happy relationship with your husband when there is conflict on such basic things."

"Oh, there you are wrong, Mother," Perpetua exclaimed, caught up in her new enthusiasm, "for the advice that I have read in Tertullian will make me a better wife, I know."

Claudia said nothing — she always found it hard to talk to her daughter — but she wondered privately if one could really find the answers to love and marriage in a book.

Now Perpetua impatiently brushed from her mind the talk of the other prisoners in the room as she mentally stiffened her own resolve. How could they speak about whether it was harder to live as a Christian or to die as a Christian when that made no difference at all? All that mattered was to *be* a Christian and nothing within one's self or outside one's self could be allowed to change that fact.

The voice of the centurion sounded suddenly and heavily in the little room. "There is a prisoner here by the name of Vivia Perpetua?"

Perpetua turned and saw the centurion standing in the doorway with her father. They could hardly see into the darkness so she came quickly forward and greeted her father, but she was doubtful if she should embrace him, not knowing how he would receive her. However, he embraced her warmly and spoke with sorrow at seeing her in such a dismal prison.

"How is it, my daughter, that you did not deny this charge and demand to be brought to the test at once? But I have found you now, thanks to Mark, and there will speedily be an end to this incarceration."

"Father," Perpetua said without preface, "I cannot deny the charge."

Aelianus was shocked and stunned into silence as he realized the meaning of her words. His look changed from one of concern and affection to disbelief and consternation.

"Do you mean to say you are a Christian?" He was still incredulous.

"Father, do you see this waterpot? You call it *urceolum*, do you not? You could never call it by any other name because that is what it is. No more can I be called anything other than Christian, because that is what I am. I am a Christian!" Her words were ringing and clear, an indirect reproach to the doubts and qualms voiced by the other prisoners earlier.

Aelianus with difficulty controlled his anger at this unequivocal declaration and tried to speak calmly as a parent to a rebellious child.

"Have you no thought for your parents then? All I have done for you, yes, to my sorrow, I even favored you more than your brothers. And is this how you repay me? Have you no consideration either for your mother or your infant son who cannot live without you? Will you throw away everything for a name?"

"Do not forget, Father, that you also disregarded your safety and the safety of your family when you would not be silent in the corruption of the emperor's court. I would be false to my own father if I were not true to my conscience at whatever cost."

"Your analogy is completely false, daughter. I spoke out against vice and corruption. You are allied with it."

Now it was Perpetua's turn to grow angry. "There you are altogether wrong. Our master taught us dictates of morality, honesty, and integrity that parallel and go far beyond

those of Marcus Aurelius. We honor our parents, give kindness and charity to all, respect lawful authority — "

"No," Aelianus interrupted. "There's the difference. I know
nothing of your other virtues but you do not respect authority or you would do the one thing that is asked of you —
make the sacrifice to the gods."

"But we do everything else. We pay taxes, the Christian
soldiers fight for the empire, we obey all the laws, we pray
for the emperor, but this one thing God will not permit — to
make sacrifices to false gods."

"This one thing he will not permit — *now*. So you defy
the law in one respect and what will it be next? Or should
the lawmakers consult with your 'god' and ask him whether
their laws satisfy him before they enact them? And where
will they find him to ask? They'd have to ask all the priests,
I suppose, and get a hundred different answers! The government can't be administered that way. The authorities have
to decide what is best and proper for the state and proceed
from there. Otherwise Rome is lost."

"Then if Rome will not recognize and listen to the one
true God, Rome should be lost!"

Aelianus' jaw dropped in amazement, and he looked at
her with the horror and disgust one reserves for unclean
things that fatten on carrion and offal. He raised his hand
as if he would strike her, but his hand fell to his side and he
turned slowly away. His silence was more harsh in condemnation than any rebuke, and Perpetua searched for words to
take away the sting of her outburst, to explain her beliefs,
to make him understand. But Aelianus, without looking at
her again, left the room abruptly, and from that day until
the day of the trial Perpetua saw her father no more.

WHEN Aelianus returned to Mark and Gaius in the back room of Saturninus' shop, his bearing and words showed clearly that his anger at his daughter's stubbornness overrode any parental concern over her future fate.

"She has obstinately refused to deny that she is a . . ." His tongue balked at the word and he shook his head as if to rid himself of all the abominable connotations of it. He turned away without speaking more and stared back at the blank wall of Balbus' house and the door that had so recently closed behind him.

His whole life — all that he had suffered and lived for — all this she would kick and trample underfoot with no more concern than she would crush a spider. He could still hear her words, strong and ringing, "Rome should be lost!" Just where did she think she would be if Rome were lost? And all the rest of the Christians too? Oh yes, they enjoyed the prosperity that the Roman senators and governors worked so hard for, they enjoyed the peace the Roman soldiers fought to preserve, they traveled on the roads Roman engineers and Roman money built — yes, that very leisure and freedom that she used to study these insane ideas was given to her by Rome. For the good life she had, the honorable marriage — that she owed to the Roman administration under which he had been able to amass a small fortune, not once, but twice.

Was that the trouble? Too much money? Too much leisure? He had been very indulgent toward her — he had to admit it. Perhaps he had fostered that very pride and willfulness she showed today. She had certainly none of the gentleness of spirit of her mother. Perhaps it was his fault for the way he had brought her up. He had been much stricter with his sons, and they showed a more restrained and sensible attitude, Mark especially. Gaius — well, he was still young, and he must make sure to straighten out some of his ideas.

He turned to them now — they were entitled to some explanation. He could see the distress in their faces. This disgrace would be hard on all of them.

"I would never have believed it," he began, "if I hadn't heard it with my own ears. It is really true, she is a Christian — my own daughter! And she is not blinded or misguided — she is well aware of what it means. She has set herself up boldly in defiance of Rome. I wouldn't soil my lips repeating to you the terrible treasonous words she uttered! When she said those words I could hardly keep from chastising her myself. If she had still been under my authority, I would have punished her on the spot."

Mark felt that some comment was required. He did not have to feign his dismay at the revelation by his father, for his distress was every bit as deep-seated, although from a different cause. He must find some way to be alone, to come to grips with this problem in his own mind.

"Father, may I have your permission to stay in the city and try to see her myself?" he asked.

"It will do no good. She is adamant. I don't know who or what has bewitched her. She certainly didn't get it from Novius. Well, stay if you wish, Mark. I must go home and take this dreadful news to your mother."

Mark was in a fever of impatience for his father and Gaius to leave, for he felt his control would not hold much longer. His father's own agitation had so far prevented him from noticing anything strange, but emotions were boiling so furiously within him now that reason and caution were no longer in command.

At last the door closed behind them and Mark listened without a breath for the tinkling of the bell that indicated that they had left the shop. Then he let out his breath in an explosive sigh and sank to the table, burying his face in his hands as a flood of horrifying thoughts engulfed him.

Felicity — Felicity — he saw her as he had seen her last, frail and helpless and easily wearied in her pregnancy. Felicity thrown into a terrible prison, manhandled by bestial soldiers, exposed to ridicule and abuse and trial before everyone! Felicity torn to pieces by wild beasts! How could God take any pleasure in such a frightful sacrifice? No, no, no, it must not be! He felt torn with rebellion and bitterness.

But he had no right. No right to be bitter, or to turn on God for abandoning her to this brutal and inhuman fate. He had abandoned her first. Why had he ever let her go? Let her go? He hadn't let her go — he had never even made a move toward her! What demon of indecision had kept him immobile when every fiber of his being ached for her!

How small and delicate she had seemed the day he had carried her so gently in his arms after preventing her rape in the garden shed! He could see again the wild black cascade of her hair over his arm, and on her cheek one blue vein like a single stroke of an artist's brush marking the whiteness of her skin. How his unsuspected love had burst that day into a wild and impossible longing! How it overwhelmed him even now — and he had no right! No right even to think of her suffering in the way he was.

Why had he delayed so long, weighing with his damnable deliberation the difficulties in the way of marriage to a slave and his own hesitancy to break a personal vow to God? Why had he not acted at once as soon as he knew his feelings? But — he had told himself — there was plenty of time, she was very young, he could wait a year and he would know better. Could it be infatuation? So she had gone — left with Perpetua, to go to that house, to be forced into marriage, to be brought to this frightful jeopardy.

And what had he gained by his caution? She had left, but his turmoil had not left, and he found it impossible to study, to pray. Why had he not spoken when he learned she was to be married? He had said to himself it was a sign from God that he was meant to live celibate — Cowardice! Cowardice! He feared a showdown with Novius and his father — that was the truth of it. He could have saved her from an unwanted marriage. He could have saved her from this peril if he had had the courage to take her away.

And even now she belonged to another and yet he was consumed with such a passion that he knew himself both unworthy and unwilling to follow the calling for which he had so unmanned himself.

❖ ❖ ❖

The door opened and Irene came in with bread and fruit and wine. Mark was glad of this interruption, glad to exchange the tense and involved emotions with his family and his own almost despairing self-recrimination for the quiet of a stranger who was yet a friend. The food he saw was but an excuse, for she ate little, for companionship only. But her need to talk was great, for she had been alone since the day before, not caring or daring to go outside her house.

"I can't understand why I wasn't arrested too, Mark," she began. "Saturninus and Secundulus were in this room waiting for Saturus to come, but almost the minute that your sister and the others arrived, the soldiers entered at the back and arrested them. They gave no explanation and wouldn't even talk to me. Then they swiftly hustled them over to Balbus'. Doesn't it seem strange to you that they took only these and didn't even wait for the priest?"

"It's not really strange," Mark explained, from his wider experience and knowledge. "The authorities have followed many different procedures in dealing with Christians. Sometimes they make a practice of arresting only catechumens with the idea that they can be more easily induced to apostatize. They are coming to realize that in many cases the courage and steadfastness of the martyrs publicizes rather than discourages the spread of Christianity."

"That's what Saturus thought. He arrived not long after they were arrested and immediately went to the praetorium to give himself up so that he could be with them, to encourage them, and to baptize them if they were willing. But," she puzzled, "how would the soldiers know whom to seize? That presupposes an informer or spy, doesn't it?"

"We wouldn't have to look very far," Mark agreed, "considering the position Perpetua's husband has in the government."

"Her husband! You mean her husband may have authorized this? Why, I can't believe it!"

"Well, he put on a good act last night of knowing nothing,

but it rang hollow to me. There's a great deal I can't understand about this, but I think Novius is involved."

"Does this mean that it is perhaps a personal matter?" Irene wondered with a little shred of hope. "Could it be possible that since they are being held privately it is just for a scare or a warning and they will not be prosecuted further?"

"It is possible, I suppose. I wish I could believe it. But after seeing Novius this morning I don't think he will be satisfied with a warning. I think it more likely he wants to get in the clear, so to speak, before it is made public. He spoke of divorcing Perpetua. If he does, I think there is no hope for them. The regular channels of the law will take over, and if they refuse to sacrifice, they will be condemned."

"Saturninus will never sacrifice, I know," Irene said quietly. "He has already given up so much for his faith. Let me show you something." She went to a cupboard and brought out a gleaming bronze statuette of a mother and child. It was full of action — the mother tossing her child high so that the curve of her arms and the curve of the baby perfectly expressed her lilting joy.

"We had to be content with bronze children — all the babies I have brought into the world and all the babies he has made — yet we have never had one of our own."

"This is an exquisite thing," Mark exclaimed, for it was far superior to the dull and lifeless statues commonly seen in Carthaginian shops. "When did Saturninus make it?"

"He made it for me as a present for Saturnalia two years ago. He intended then to have copies made and sell them as Leto and Apollo. You can't sell anything unless you put gods' names on them, but he really just loved to copy the human figure in all its forms. After he made something he'd pick out an appropriate name. But this one never was marketed. He started taking instructions and of course had to give up his business. Saturus insisted that he destroy all the pagan statues. He melted down the bronzes and sold it in bars, but the terra-cotta ones he crushed with a sledgehammer. He couldn't eat for two days. This one I hid. After all, it had never been named. Do you think it is really pagan?"

Mark turned the statuette in his hands, noting how the soft curves of the flesh revealed themselves beneath the thin garments. It was very human and very beautiful. Perhaps it was pagan too.

"It is lovely," he compromised. "You will always be glad you have it."

Irene put the statuette away and sat down again across the table from Mark. "You are worried about your sister?" she asked.

"Well, no," he hesitated. Her warmth and confidences encouraged frankness. "I am more worried about Felicity. You know how it is with her. They cannot execute her now, for Roman law forbids the execution of a woman who is with child, but they can hold her in prison until the child is born. Won't she suffer dreadfully under those circumstances?"

"Not necessarily," Irene answered. "Comfortable surroundings are no help when a woman comes into labor. She can be delivered as safely on a prison floor as in the most sumptuous villa, nor is she likely to suffer any more. What you should do, I think, is to try to end this secrecy if possible and get permission to visit them. You must know many officials. Why don't you go to see them and try to get someone interested in their behalf? You might be able to get it out into the open and then we could be of some help."

82

Mark was glad to have positive action suggested and spent the few hours remaining in the day calling on officials and acquainting them with the arrest of his sister. Though for the most part he was courteously received, no one would offer any help when they learned the charge against Perpetua, excepting only Crispus, who had so kindly given hospitality to the Vivians that day. He promised to see the governor and try to find out what could be done.

But as it happened his efforts were not necessary. According to schedule a merchant ship, the *Falcon,* sailed the following morning for Rome and after that the prisoners were brought openly to the main prison.

XII

Before the prisoners were moved from Balbus' storeroom, Saturus joined them. It was not immediately apparent to them that he was also a prisoner, although he was escorted by soldiers, since he strode into the room in his usual vigorous manner and he seemed rather to lead the soldiers than to be led by them.

Saturus, though not tall, was broad of build with a massive head made more striking by thick brown hair worn longer than was customary. This, combined with the largeness of his features, gave him almost an untidy look, yet it seemed as if his body, large as it was, could not contain his spirit, so did the force of his personality flow out, reaching, reaching toward everyone he met. And this even before he spoke. His voice was deep and strong and so vibrant with feeling and expressive in range that it attracted and held the attention of anyone who heard him, irrespective of the words he used. His deep convictions burned in the heartfelt tones and compelled belief in his sincerity.

Now, when he spoke, the voice filled the little room and boomed out into the kitchen as well, and it was as heady and challenging as the roll of a drum. But the words were quiet.

"Peace! Peace be with you, my children!" and he blessed them all with a large and open sign of the cross.

"I'm so thankful you were able to get permission to visit us, Father," Perpetua began, greatly relieved to see him after the trying interview with her father.

But Saturus' laugh rumbled out low and deep. "I am not a visitor, Perpetua. I am a prisoner like yourselves. I am here to share your fate whatever it may be."

If the sight and sound of Saturus had brought heart to the prisoners, this news lifted their spirits still more. His very openness of manner helped to dispel the shadows and resolve their confusion.

"But how did it happen that you were arrested, Father? Are there others as well?" Saturninus asked, fearing for his wife.

"I arrived at your house only a very short time after your arrest," Saturus explained. "Your wife told me what had happened and I immediately went to the praetorium and demanded to be arrested with you. Strangely enough, no one knew anything about your arrest there. Nor apparently was there any general order for arrest of Christians, because I kept insisting I was a Christian, yet no one would take the responsibility for arresting me. I remained until nightfall and was at last forced to leave.

"In the morning I returned and continued to press everyone I could obtain speech with for information. At last I was taken to a tribune who seemed to know more than the rest and he obliged by putting me under arrest. A very intelligent young man, extremely interested in Christianity. He questioned me most searchingly and seemed better informed than most Romans of his class. So many of them believe the lies that have been told attributing to us all the crimes of which the pagans themselves are guilty, but he had rather the opposite idea.

" 'Love,' he said, 'you Christians talk about love, yet you forbid it. You say you love everyone with the result that you love nobody.'

" 'Oh, but you are wrong,' I assured him. 'You are confusing love and lust. It is only lust we forbid.'

" 'And is the love of a man for his wife lust?'

"Well, you can see how confused he was, yet he listened intently to my explanations, and I really believe if I had had more time I might have been able to convert him. As it was, we discussed religion almost the whole day and I hardly noticed the passage of time.

"Yet it is here that I wanted to be, with you" — he put aside these other speculations abruptly — "because I would not have you go to your trial without the grace of baptism. And let us not delay any longer, for we do not know how much time we may have."

Perpetua was grateful that he had turned so suddenly to the subject of baptism. When he began to speak, she had wanted to ask him if he had seen the tribune Novius, but, as he continued, she no longer wanted to ask — nor did she need.

Felicity on the contrary was not glad to have the subject of baptism brought up. Filled with fears for her unborn child and encouraged by Revocatus' declaration, she kept deep inside of her a small hope that somehow they two might evade this sacrifice of their lives. It was too sudden, she should have time to think. It was hard to speak now because Saturus had heartened and freshened their spirits so, just as the infrequent north wind freshens a day in autumn, but in the same way he seemed to catch up and carry all before him as if they had no will of their own. Yet she must speak.

"Father," she hesitated, not knowing how to continue. How do you refuse to be baptized? "I can't. . . . I just can't go on. I can't condemn my baby to death. How can I do that? Surely God would not want that. What can I do?"

"I'm sorry, Felicity, that you didn't know this," Saturus answered, filled with pity that she had been troubled so unnecessarily. "This decision is not asked of you. You have been worried about something that will not happen. It is against Roman law to execute a mother who is with child. Your baby will be born and someone will raise it for you if it must come to that. They are Romans, not barbarians. You don't have to worry about your child."

Secundulus spoke now. The five of them had talked in whispers ever since they had been arrested because of the open doorway, and the old man found Saturus' loud voice startling and a little frightening. "Father, wouldn't it be better if you spoke more quietly so that the soldiers will not come in and prevent you from baptizing us?"

"Oh, by no means, Secundulus," boomed Saturus. "We need worry no longer about concealment. We are already discovered. What more can we fear? But now while we can, let us show ourselves openly as we are and sweep away as much of the tissue of falsity as we can. Those men outside are soldiers by profession, but first of all they are men, men for whom Christ our Savior died even as for you and me. Let us rather invite them in. Who knows what good may come of it? There will surely be no harm."

He went to the doorway and spoke to the centurion and the soldiers.

"Sirs, I've no doubt you've heard many things about

Christians, mostly false, but some true. You know that we go to our death cheerfully rather than give up our faith, and you have no doubt heard that we indulge in all kinds of vicious and depraved practices. Which is the truth? Are you not curious to know? Do you really think any man will die because he loves evil or crime so much he will not give it up? Will he go to his death because he will not give up stealing or lechery or drunkenness?

"You are soldiers and you know what it is to face death. Why do you die? For your pleasures? But if you die, you can no longer enjoy them. For money? If you die, you will never receive it. You fight for your pay but why do you not run from death? It is because you cannot deny your inner manhood. You die because you must protect your honor, and courage, and worth. No one goes willingly to death except for something that is good.

"But, as for these wicked and vicious practices, you will have a chance to see for yourself. I am going to baptize these prisoners. They are not yet Christians but up to this time have been studying and learning. By baptism they are made Christians. Baptism is never seen by those who are not Christians, but you can see it now and discover for yourselves if these rites are depraved or immoral."

His words were so disarming that the centurion saw no reason to object and did indeed out of curiosity step inside the room though he motioned the guards to remain outside. Inside or outside, they could not escape the vibrant voice of Saturus and the compelling power of his words.

"What is baptism?" the priest began, and his explanation was as new to the catechumens as it was to the strangers. "By baptism we are made Christians. But even more than that, we are made men. We are freed from our bondage to earth by an outpouring of divinity so that we can rise to the greatest nobility that the human spirit can achieve. By baptism we are given a share in divine life and, joined with God, we can perfect the dignity of man."

Saturus lifted the heavy waterpot and carried it to the center of the room. "We have no running water, so we must use what we have. I cannot lift this with one hand," he told the prisoners, "so you must bow low to receive the water upon your foreheads. In the same way we must bend down our pride and accept the whole of this life willingly, and with life, death, the cross. Water, the symbol of life, is never destroyed. It flows unceasingly, it rises into the air as vapor, it descends as rain, it never loses its essence, its being. So our life, at once cut and blessed by the sign of the cross, is not destroyed but changed and renewed."

Saturus directed the men to take off their outer garment and the women their veils. The torn remnant of Felicity's veil was lying in a corner to dry after she had rinsed the blood out of it. I have nothing to lay aside, she thought, except my reluctance.

"In this way," Saturus explained, "we lay aside the sins and errors of our past and enter into a new life, a life patterned after our divine Model, Jesus Christ. Even as he did, we accept in this new life the cross while he offers to us the crown of life everlasting."

One by one each of the prisoners knelt before him and bowed low so that the priest might tip the waterpot three times with one hand and make the sign of the cross while repeating the words of baptism. After all had been baptized, Saturus blessed the garments which had been laid aside and gave them again to their owners.

"You do not have new garments, but these have been

cleansed by your sufferings for your faith. Put them on, as if they were pure white garments, and pray with me that prayer you now have the right to say. You have said this prayer many times before, but now you are truly children of God and can rightly use the address — Our Father."

Speaking the words of the Lord's Prayer together with the magnetic voice of Saturus, all felt the shadows vanish and the walls retreat and the soldiers lose their menace. It was not until much, much later and all the others slept that the doubts crept back to Felicity's mind. Carried along by the eloquence and enthusiasm of the priest and the ready acquiescence of her companions, she had not realized that while Saturus put to rest her fears about her unborn child, her unwillingness went deeper than that.

Oh, dear God, she thought, I love this life too much to leave it! Here I have come at last to some measure of human happiness. Can I not now enjoy it?

She wished she could reach out and stop the spinning on of time, but instead it seemed to move faster and faster, sweeping her, confused and unready, to the moment of decision. And on her Revocatus had placed the choice. She must decide for them both. How could she ask for death?

Yet in real truth, how could she deny God and live? It was only the revelation of God and the acceptance of life that Claudia had disclosed to her that had brought her to the pinnacle of happiness on which she now stood. Her love was tied to the love of God and her life solely sustained by him. She could not cut herself off from God without losing everything. She knew what she must do, but she fought against it.

Was it right to feel so trapped and unwilling?

Trapped and unwilling! Those were the same words she

had used to Claudia when she went to her for comfort on learning that Perpetua's husband intended to give her to his slave Revocatus in marriage. When was that — less than a year ago? It seemed like another life. She saw herself as if she were a stranger, that night she had risen long before dawn and gone out into the silent streets of the city in utter blackness. It was still vivid in her mind, although eons ago. The moon had set and the tall buildings shut out even the dim light of the stars. She was glad of the darkness, and she hurried along the Via Diana from Novius' house near the Hill of the Temples. She saw no one and heard nothing, for her footsteps were so light that they did not arouse the challenge of the watchdogs in the buildings she passed.

The darkness and the silence of the city gave her a strange eerie feeling, something like the mood that would come over her as she watched the ocean at night — a feeling of sadness and longing and an overpowering sense of mystery that both attracted and frightened her.

How different had the city seemed when they first came here to live! Then it had been exciting, noisy, full of interesting things and people. She loved it all after the quiet of the country. Novius would often give her a denarius to spend for herself, and she would spend hours in the market looking over all the strange things offered for sale before she decided what to buy. There were fewer slaves in Novius' household, but there was much less work for her to do, since she did nothing but attend to Perpetua's wishes.

The city slaves had more freedom to come and go than those in the country, and they were more sophisticated and copied the pleasures of their masters. Felicity gradually acquired a few pieces of jewelry which she liked to look at, although she never wore them because Perpetua would not permit jewelry either for herself or for her slave.

The house too was always interesting. It was never quiet when Novius was home. He often had friends in for dinner and these dinners lasted far into the night with much drinking and boisterousness. Perpetua sometimes was hostess to smaller quieter groups so that few were the evenings they spent alone. Even then Novius had to be home for only five minutes before the whole house was in an uproar. He could stage a mock fight with the dogs, badger the cook, tease Felicity, and start an argument with Perpetua in less time than it would take another man to unlace his sandals.

Felicity rather enjoyed the teasing at first — the hilarity was quite a contrast to the soberness of the Villa Vivia — and she did like having a little money to spend for the first time in her life. But the teasing slipped gradually into a flirtation, still very casual and open, and Felicity could see it angered Perpetua so that she began to be uneasy. After Perpetua became pregnant and rested more often, Novius would surprise Felicity or waylay her in the hall. Felicity knew it was nothing serious to him, but what was not serious to him could be to her and certainly was to Perpetua. But she didn't dare mention these secret encounters to her mistress.

The evening she found herself alone in the house with Novius she was dreadfully uneasy, because she knew he had deliberately planned it that way. Then he insisted that she sit down with him as if they were equals and he gave her more and more wine to drink until she was completely befuddled. She had not really been afraid of him, even though he was the master and she the slave, because she did not think he would try to take her against her will. But now she found herself so addlepated and leaden-limbed that she could hardly make known her objections. And they were actually reclining and Novius' hand was within the upper folds of her tunic when Perpetua returned. Her face grew hot under her mantle as she remembered it, though Perpetua had never blamed her or even mentioned the incident afterward.

And now there was this — this hateful marriage planned for her!

How glad she was to leave that house this morning in the darkness! How she wished she could keep walking and walking and walking and never return!

She had left the city behind now as the dawn was breaking and she passed many farmers and slaves bringing their produce to market in their carts. She kept her mantle wrapped about her with only her eyes showing, for the air was still cool and — this was the real reason — she hated her own appearance. How she wished she had not been born a woman! How she wished she had been born ugly!

When at last she reached her former home her eyes filled with tears and a lump came into her throat at seeing the familiar courtyard and Claudia sitting spinning. Beside her the ornamental pool was dotted with fresh flowers. It was Claudia's delight to keep many bright and fragrant flowers floating on the clear waters. They retained their freshness and fragrance for a long time and their mobility made them perpetually interesting to watch. Felicity had never seen this done in any other home. When they entertained at night they would float lamps in intricately carved wooden ships which Aelianus had discovered in a little shop in Carthage.

Felicity sat down at Claudia's feet and asked no other

refreshment than to be home again. Now she poured out the whole story of this proposed marriage, how strongly Perpetua opposed it, and how reluctant she herself was.

"I feel so trapped and unwilling," she burst out. "Where can I go for help?"

"Why are you so unwilling?" Claudia asked. "Do you hate this man then?"

"But you know him, mistress," Felicity began, a little surprised that she would have to explain. The man's repulsiveness seemed only too evident. "He is so ugly, he is like a brute."

"Yes, he is ugly. No one could deny that. But are you going to reject someone simply because God didn't give him attractive features? You are beautiful, Felicity, but what joy has your beauty ever given you?"

Felicity could not answer, thinking of her wish as she had walked through the dawn that she had been born ugly. She continued more uncertainly.

"But I am afraid of him. You have seen him, mistress. He looks like a man who might do anything."

"Yes, I have seen him, Felicity," Claudia's voice was full of compassion. "He looks like a man who has suffered very much."

Felicity was taken aback, suddenly seeing Revocatus in a different light altogether, as a fellow human being deserving of sympathy, rather than a monster to be feared. He had really never given her any cause to fear him, for he had never injured her or even said a single unkind word. She was ashamed of her thoughts and suspicions of him, but she made one last attempt to explain her reluctance.

"Perpetua said that Novius took him from the quarry

gang and that only desperate criminals were sent there —
murderers and the like."

"Only a few years ago, Felicity, Christians were also sent
to the quarries. They were called desperate criminals and
accused of all kinds of crimes without proof. Are you going
to condemn Revocatus without proof? The only crime we
know he was guilty of was love of liberty. It was for this
crime that he was beaten and branded and chained. What
kind of a Christian are you, Felicity? Can you not find it
in your heart to pity this man?"

Felicity was silent, confused. She was grateful to Claudia
for speaking so bluntly, for she had certainly been a long
way from the faith she professed when she had given in
to feelings of abhorrence toward one of her fellowmen.
She was supposed to love even her enemies, but Revocatus
had never given her any cause to consider him an enemy.
When she thought of the sufferings he must have experienced to have made him, while still young, appear so
brutal, she was truly filled with pity.

Pity, yes — but marriage? . . .

Then Claudia continued more gently, holding the girl's
hand in hers. "You are not afraid of Revocatus, Felicity,
you are afraid of marriage. Because of the violence used
against you, you fear your womanhood. But it is a strange
thing that this same faculty which it is so outrageous to
take by violence can lead to the most perfect happiness
when willingly surrendered. And this is as true in marriage
as out of it. You will be happy only insofar as you give
willingly.

"Don't, Felicity, don't say that you are trapped and unwilling. Go to your marriage freely and willingly. Give

yourself. Love this man that no one has ever loved before. You will forget yourself and you will find a happiness you would not otherwise have ever known."

Claudia had been right. The counsel Felicity had thought difficult had proved easy.

Trapped and unwilling. . . . Now again she used those words. Trapped by her own selfishness? Unwilling to give completely?

XIII

MARK did not try to get in to see the prisoners in the same way his father had done. Driven by a need to absolve himself of the cowardice of which he was convicted in his own eyes, he wanted to show his interest openly as much as possible and to jeopardize his own safety in any way short of absolute confession. Each centurion he saw, each soldier he questioned he felt linked him more closely to the prisoners and to their fate. He even went directly to the governor's residence and tried to obtain an interview, declaring openly to his secretary that he wished to see him about the Christian prisoners, that he was the brother of one of those arrested, and that he requested permission to see her. The governor kept him waiting for three hours and then did not see him — Mark would have been surprised if he had — but he did write a brief note to the jailer of the prison to which the prisoners had by this time been transferred, authorizing Mark's admission to see his sister.

The city prison was located on the top of a hill south of the wharves in the roughest section of Carthage. The hill rose steeply out of the flat land around it, barren and craggy and unnatural. It was actually a huge pile of rubble, the remnants of old fortifications which had been collected in this one spot when the walls of Carthage were demolished, never to be rebuilt. Nothing would grow on this place and it was ugly and gray and dirty. The bleak almost windowless prison fortress squatted on its top, glooming over the slums below. As Mark approached the hill through the thinning crowds of sailors and workmen in the heat just after midday, he thought with pity of the long two-mile walk the prisoners had made from the forum with this desperate and forbidding hill at the end.

The prison had been built for maximum security and was administered by one jailer with the assistance of two guards who were actually caretaker and cook. The military had nothing to do with the prisoners once they were admitted here.

The jailer admitted Mark with respect when he saw the governor's signature on the order and unlocked the door to a very small dark cell, furnished only with two thin pallets and a stool. Perpetua faced the door as it opened, standing as straight as if weariness or fear were unknown to her. Mark felt a thrill of pride to see how resolute and indomitable was her bearing.

"Mark," she exclaimed, with relief, for she didn't know what to expect when the door opened. "How glad I am to see you!" Then she remembered Saturus. "You're not a prisoner too, are you?"

"No," Mark reassured her, "by the grace of God, not yet. I have the governor's permission to see you. What a foul place! Felicity — how is she?"

He could see her now, crumpled on a pallet, still and broken, as if all will to live or move had been wrung out of her. Her face was gray and covered with perspiration, but her hand was cold when he touched it. She did not move or open her eyes.

"Let her sleep, Mark. She has not slept for more than two hours since we were arrested, and I don't know how she managed to walk here from the forum. Revocatus had to carry her up the hill."

"She doesn't look as if she is just sleeping, Perpetua. I can hardly feel any pulse." He shouted out the small window in the door, for the jailer had locked it after admitting him.

"There's a woman desperately sick in here. You'd better bring blankets quickly if you don't want to be called to account for the way you take care of your prisoners."

"What's this? What's this? Another one?" The jailer unlocked the door and came over to the pallet where Felicity lay. "What can I do?" he complained. "The soldiers deliver them half dead and I get the blame if they die on my hands." He felt for Felicity's pulse and then called the guard.

"Bring blankets and hot bricks. We'll have to try to rouse her. The men called for help as soon as they were brought in. The old man has a high fever and chills. We have been trying to help him. No one said there was any difficulty in here."

"Whether they said anything or not," Mark charged him, "there is no excuse for leaving them in this damp hole with nothing to rest on, no blankets or coverings, no food, no drink. Are you setting yourself up as judge and sentencing them to death yourself? You saw her condition. Do you know that if anything happens to her before the baby is born, you could be prosecuted for murder?"

"Now, now, master, it's not my doing. It was the march the soldiers forced them to make. I can't be held responsible."

"I will personally see that you *are* held responsible," Mark thundered. "And you had better see that more comfortable quarters are available as soon as she can be moved." Mark was oblivious of the fact that he was in no position to order anyone around, and his assurance made the jailer forget that too.

The warmth of the blankets and the hot bricks at her feet slowly roused Felicity from the state of shock she was in. She awakened to the sound of Mark's angry words. She recognized his voice without opening her eyes and it made her feel safe and comfortable. It is all a bad dream, she thought. When I open my eyes I will find myself home again. She enjoyed for a little while feeling herself a child again, hearing Mark's voice as his voice and Perpetua's and Claudia's had filled her childhood — filled it with kindness and affection to take the place of the mother love she had never missed. Her eyelids felt pressed down by a drowsy contentment and she was unwilling to make any effort to raise them.

But gradually with greater awareness she could distinguish Mark's words and catch the worried anxiety in his voice and slowly and reluctantly she opened her eyes. Before her the prison walls loomed up gray and damp, but Mark, bending over her, sighed with relief and pressed her hand, and she was surprised to find that the feeling of contentment did not evaporate. So peaceful had been her slipping away and so gentle her recall that for the first time since the nightmare of the arrest and imprisonment she was vibrantly aware of God's presence about her.

The jailer as he saw the woman recovering, was suddenly conscious of his responsibility for security, since the door to the cell had been left open during the crisis, and he now ordered Mark to leave. But when Mark protested he had still not had his visit with his sister, he reluctantly granted him a quarter hour more with the door locked.

Perpetua was full of questions about her baby but Mark could not give her much information since he had not been home after he had ridden back to the city with the money on the morning after the arrest. She was somewhat reassured that her mother was taking care of the child, but still not completely satisfied, for her own longing and need of him was as great as her concern.

"If only I could have him with me, Mark," she said. "Do you think you could ask?"

"You mean you'd want him here in this dismal place?"

"As long as possible, I would like to have him with me, Mark. You can understand, can't you? That is all I ask now. As long as God wills."

"I'll see, Perpetua. It is easier to deal with this fellow than with the military. You will have to know, Perpetua, you can expect no help from Novius. He told us that he intended to get a divorce." He couldn't bring himself to tell her about the threat to repudiate his son.

She did not seem surprised. "How did you find out, Mark? Did he tell you that we had been arrested?"

"He came out to the villa with Publius the night you were arrested. He wanted us to believe that he didn't know where you were, but that he suspected you of abandoning the baby and leaving him. We didn't find out that you had been arrested until the following morning when a centurion met him and told him."

"Are we the only ones arrested, Mark?"

"So far as I know. I was not questioned about my faith all the time I was inquiring about you."

"You know, Mark, we were arrested so soon after we arrived at Saturninus' shop that it seemed almost as if we had been followed. From the beginning I thought that my husband must have known about it from his close association with the governor, but now I wonder if he — I'm afraid he might — oh Mark, do you suppose he could have *planned* it?"

For the first time her control broke and she put her head on his shoulder and wept unashamedly. He comforted her, gently, wordlessly, his heart aching for her torment. He wished he could give her some reassurance, but he didn't know what to say. The same suspicion had been in his mind, and she knew Novius better than he. Yet he could see what a dreadful canker this thought would be and how much harder it would be for her to face the situation if this bitterness were added to it.

"Try not to think about it, little sister." He used the affectionate name he had called her when they were growing up together. "This could not have happened through any human agency, unless it were God's will. Now I'll talk to the jailer and if I can get his permission, I'll bring Publius back as quickly as I can ride. Please, little sister, put these suspicions from your mind. Now I must go." The jailer was unlocking the door. He kissed her again and bent over Felicity to say good-bye.

"Good-bye, Felicity. You must eat well and rest and have good heart."

"I will," Felicity promised with a faint smile.

Perpetua promised nothing. What could she promise? She could put these suspicions out of her mind just as easily as she could tell the wind to stop blowing or the sea to be calm or the sun to fall out of the sky. But she felt cold all over at the thought of the ugly diabolical hatred which they disclosed. She shouldn't have put it into words, she should have kept the cover on this yawning pit filled with all the demons of hell. Could her own husband plot her death and Felicity's in such a dreadful manner and with such cold-blooded connivance?

After her conversion she had shown him all the kindness and gentleness of which she was capable, for she knew that she was overly proud and willful. Her tongue was sharp and quick and Novius was ever ready to engage her in verbal combat. These sparrings had become increasingly bitter because of their unsatisfactory intimacy. Conscious of the difficulty she had determined to refuse every challenge and to turn aside the battles at the beginning with a conciliatory response. She was submissive to him in every way, though she prayed and hoped that she could win him from being such a slave to his passions. It was unfair, she knew, to condemn him for being a pagan, though pagans could live temperately too, as her father did. Yet she never refused him even after she had become pregnant though it was against her better judgment.

Never that is, until the night that she had discovered the full extent of his grossness —

She remembered every word that had been spoken that night as if they had been burned on her mind. She had started out alone in the litter to go to her parents' house for dinner. Novius had said he had to see the governor that evening so he was not able to go. Felicity usually attended her mistress wherever she went but for some reason brought up by Novius did not go this time. Perpetua was provoked at her husband because it was her mother's birthday, and she thought he could have made more of an effort to accompany her or at least to see that Felicity could go since her mother loved so much to see her.

They had been gone about half an hour, for it was slow going through the crowds in the city, when she recalled that she had forgotten to bring a woolen mantle that Felicity had woven for Claudia. She might not have returned even then, except that she had been driven by a strange uneasiness.

When she entered the house she noticed a light coming from the dining room and was surprised since Novius had intended to take his dinner with the governor. She went there at once, thinking that his plans might have been changed and he would be able to go with her after all. But she stopped short in the doorway, transfixed by what she saw. It was no dinner, but a scene of debauchery! Wine and wine cups only on the table and Novius reclining — with Felicity on the couch beside him!

He could at least have had the grace to look ashamed, she thought, reliving her shock.

"Well, my dear wife." He laughed when he saw her, but he did remove his arm from around Felicity. He looked very strange and reckless, drunk with something other than wine. "Felicity, go and get another cup for your mistress. She would join our festivities."

"Just go to your room, Felicity," Perpetua ordered. She noticed that the girl walked very unsteadily. She felt as if she were turned to ice. Of all people, Felicity! Coldly she sent a slave to take a message to her parents that she was ill and unable to come.

"You needn't take it out on Felicity, dear," Novius said carelessly. "She was very unwilling. I don't know how much wine I had to give her. And at that I think she would have been sick before she became amorous. Prehaps I should have tried one of those African love potions instead." He paused to give his next words more effect. "Somehow I don't seem to have much attraction for the women in my household —" He still did not rise, but took a draft of wine and ignored her as she stood regarding him with fury and contempt.

"How can you be so base?" she exclaimed. "Have you no shame, no consideration at all for me?"

Now Novius did put down his cup and rise and come toward her. "She is a very pretty little thing, Perpetua. You shouldn't leave a plate of luscious food in front of a starving man." He was not mocking now, but she could not understand what he meant.

"But I have never denied you, Novius. I have suffered you even now whenever you wished." How could he put her on the defensive like that!

"You speak so true. You have suffered me and suffered me and suffered me! Resist me, hate me, love me, anything, but suffer me no more!"

"How can you speak like that? I have tried so hard to be a good wife to you —"

"You have tried too hard, my dear wife. I didn't marry you because you were a sweet submissive little slave. I married you because you had intelligence and pride and a fire there inside your ice. And that fire has been awakened too. I could see it in the past few months. At the same time you began to be so gentle and kind to me. Who awakened that fire, sweet wife? You have been trying to cover something up with your gracious condescension."

"How can you speak so to me when I am carrying your child within me?"

105

"Are you indeed? I doubt it. I don't think I could ever father a child of you. You have locked yourself away from me. But who *has* reached you then?"

Was he serious? Was he mocking? What wild thing was in his mind? Or was he trying to distract her with these accusations from his own guilt?

But Perpetua would not be distracted.

"How do you dare accuse me — you whom I have found in this way, trying to take my own slave in my absence!"

"Would you prefer that I did it in your presence?"

Perpetua was not easily rendered speechless, but this thrust did it. As she thought about that night, she felt again that cold disdain was her only possible response to his unfounded accusations and vile remarks.

But had she been at fault too? Should she have listened to his suspicions more carefully? Could it be that he really believed them and was not simply using them as a screen to cover his own confusion? What if he had had her followed? She had always been careful to explain her absences, but beyond that had not worried too much. After all, she was a free woman and at liberty to come and go as she pleased. She had never thought to notice if she were being followed — the possibility had never occurred to her. Could it be that by disregarding his threats she had unwittingly been the cause of the arrest of them all?

But even if he had discovered her secret, would he have brought about their arrest? Did he desire her death that venomously? She shuddered at the thought. Had she underestimated the evil in this man? If he had plotted this, if he had schemed to bring about their bloody destruction, surely she was pitted, not against a man, but against the devil himself.

XIV

NOVIUS stood at the stern of the *Falcon* and watched Carthage slip away. With him was his friend Marius, who had spent the past year at Carthage familiarizing himself with the African side of his father's huge wheat import business. For Marius the year had been unrelieved exile, and it was with joy that he embarked this morning. Novius too was filled with an odd reckless exhilaration that many people experience when they are traveling and have left one part of their life and not yet picked up the other, and it was intensified in him by the turmoil of the past few days and his relief at leaving it behind.

They had emerged from the harbor and were scudding eastward on the bay of Carthage. The going would be slower after they rounded the peninsula and tacked northward toward Rome. The city was dazzlingly white and beautiful with the morning sun upon it. On the hill the governor's three-storied residence stood tall and stately, the gray marble of its walls gleaming in the bright light. The temples were older and the patina of the stone was soft and glowing, but the vivid colors in the friezes, indistinguishable in the distance, sparkled like jewels to crown their warm beauty. The sun threw a halo of brilliance around even the plain houses crowded below and the brightness almost hurt the eyes with its shimmering glory. Between the ship and the harbor countless small craft spread their multicolored sails, and it seemed as if a marine flower garden had sprouted in the bright blue waters.

Outside the small cabin on the ship near the place where the two travelers were standing was a bucket of slops to be thrown overboard as soon as they cleared the bay and reached the open sea. Novius walked over to the pail and seized a stale orange rind. Then striking a pose, he declaimed grandiloquently.

"Farewell, lovely, lily-white Carthage! Upon your virginal bosom a pure aromatic garland I lay in fond and tearful parting!" With these words he grandly tossed the piece of garbage onto the wake of the *Falcon*. Into the gesture he put all the distaste he felt for this cramped, proud Carthage and the well-ordered sterility of his life there. This was not the Africa he loved, with its warm sands and fierce vastness — this alien excrescence, this monstrous wart on its head — this was not the wild intoxicating Africa he savored like wine, but a stone he must spit out of his mouth lest it stick in his throat and prove to be the end of him.

Marius fell into his mood, launching into impromptu hexameters. "Tomb of sad Dido, even thy queen could not bear thy dull coldness! Passionate maid, I salute thee! You burned and I yearned for Rome's pleasures!"

Novius laughingly applauded his companion's mastery of heroic verse. "And now to Rome!" he exulted, "And I am free too! Oh, to be coming back to Rome, with money, favorable dispatches for the emperor in my wallet, and no entanglements!"

"That's the fastest divorce I ever heard of," Marius said with a grin. "How did you ever manage it?"

"It wasn't a divorce. It was a simple statement that the marriage was no marriage because it was not consummated. It can be issued by any magistrate without delay."

"I should think that would be a little hard to prove when there is a child of the marriage."

"*Not mine.*" Novius turned away abruptly to close the subject. The levity of the moment before was gone, and a hardness came into his face as he thought of this perfect revenge on his wife. By all the gods, he was fed to the teeth with her sexless purity, her stony submission! Well, this would be a hard thing for her pride to swallow to have to return to her father's house, humiliated by the test for Christianity, and raise her child a nameless bastard. Pure noble Perpetua!

Yet, for all his venom, he had had to leave; he could not bring himself to stay until the trial. Vasilius would bring him news; he was to sail as soon as the trial was over. Speed was of the essence, Novius had told Hilarion. Prompt action upon receiving the emperor's orders and an immediate report would serve the double purpose of furthering Hilarion's ambition and adding to his own prestige at Rome. Severus could not fail to be impressed by the ingenuity of the governor and his aide in ferreting out so quickly one of the secret cells of the Christian organization and discouraging the rest by swift prosecution. Seizing only the neophytes and winning them over by a show of force would actually have a stronger effect by emphasizing the firmness of the governor while maintaining the appearance of mercy in the emperor.

The voluntary surrender of Saturus was contrary to his plan but might be turned to an advantage, for Hilarion could justly claim to have seized the head and heart of the sect and could put on a grand spectacle with, as the culmination, the throwing of the priest to the beasts. The single execution would be a powerful deterrent, a forceful example to impress the emperor, yet with a minimum of bloodshed. Hilarion would make a good show of it, he had no doubt, and his own report to the emperor would bring him no little favor.

Novius still had his dowry from Perpetua. It had been a generous one, and she was in no position to reclaim it now. He was entitled to it, he thought to himself, after the deception practiced on him by giving him a wife who was a Christian. Yet he felt regret too, remembering how lovely Perpetua looked nursing the baby. Some evenings when they were together and Publius would smile and play with him, then Perpetua would soften and he could see how things might have been. . . .

But she could never forgive his dalliance with Felicity. He had thought to make her jealous, but it turned out to be a boomerang. He could never satisfy her, he thought. When he decided to marry Felicity to Revocatus, half out of spite because she had disdained him, and half to show Perpetua he didn't care about her slave, then there was more trouble. He didn't know a woman could care for a slave so much, but Perpetua vowed that Felicity was like a younger sister to her and she would never hear of such a disgraceful union. Then the more she opposed it, the more he was set upon it. In fact now he began to hold an impish thought in the back of his mind that once Felicity had a taste of the ugly slave she would turn a little more readily to the master.

What a fond hope that had been! He would never forget seeing Felicity the morning after the marriage. Her cheeks were flushed with a color unusual to her and her walk was slow and serene, full of a new awareness of womanhood. When she looked at Revocatus, her eyes held a softness he could not bear to see. If only Perpetua would look at him like that! Why did he have to care so much that he could not move her? Felicity did not matter, never had, but how it galled him now to see that the slave had obtained so easily what he with all his personableness, intelligence, and position had been unable to win — either the favor of the slave girl or the wholehearted love of his own wife.

It was then he began to half believe what he had said tauntingly to Perpetua about her having a lover, for it was easier for his pride to think that the love she withheld from him had been treacherously stolen by another man. So he had had Perpetua followed, but it was some time before he was able to find out anything. There were two rather surprising trips to the south side, but after that Perpetua was confined, and then for some three months after the baby was born she was so happy and their relationship so much improved that Novius began to think he had been mistaken after all and that his suspicions were unfounded. However, he still had one of the household slaves watching her, and now she began to make regular visits to a potter's shop near the forum. They didn't use that many pots! — it was obviously a trysting place. At last the slave was able to identify a man seen going into the shop as one he had also seen in the disreputable lodging on the south side.

The man was not even a Roman! A Syrian or Greek, the slave thought, perhaps even a Jew! Novius found this infatuation of Perpetua's hard to understand, but he was so glad to have a target for his anger that he did not trouble to analyze it. He was glad too to have found a flaw in his wife, and rather respected her the more for her lapse. All he needed was proof of her infidelity, and he would confront the two together at their rendezvous. The man he would kill if he were worthy of the sword, but Perpetua — he would at last truly make her his. She had come down to his level now and could no longer wrap her mantle of purity around herself and despise his base earthly passions.

At this point when he was poised and tense and eager for action he received the report that it was not a lover's rendezvous but a meeting of Christians that Perpetua attended. On this very same day in the late afternoon Hilarion showed him the directive of the emperor against the Christians.

"What do you make of this, Novius?" Hilarion had asked, for the wording of the order was general, simply directing the governor to take measures suitable and proper for suppression of the sect.

"Act! Act at once! Let judgment be swift, sure, and immediate and that will be the most effective for halting the Christians and for impressing the emperor."

"Do you mean arrest the known Christians, like Tertullian?"

"No, not Tertullian of all people! I can't advise you strongly enough to stay clear of him. He'd like nothing better than a public trial with an audience of all of Carthage. He was spawned in a law book and suckled on ink. He can make a fool of the finest jurists in the land. Besides, he'd undoubtedly appeal to Caesar in order to make the whole world his sounding board and the emperor wouldn't like that at all."

"What then, if, as you recommend, I should act at once?"

"If I learned anything in campaigning, it was to attack where the enemy is weak, not to wear out your troops battering against their strongest point. In this case go after those who are being instructed. Get them to deny this superstition publicly, and then it is discredited."

"Your suggestion has merit, Novius," Hilarion answered. "But what about the games, the wild beast shows that the people love so much?"

"What do you want to do, satisfy the people or follow the emperor's wishes? Have you seen these Christians die? Their faith and courage is almost frightening. They have more power in death than in life. Don't give them a chance to be heroes. Discredit them, make them appear foolish. Turn the young misguided ones away from the falsehood while they are still weak and vulnerable. Arrest them alone without their teacher. A group publicly renouncing Christianity will have more effect than an arena full of bloody executions."

"That's easy enough to advise, but where are we to find these learners — at once, as you say? I don't believe they advertise their meetings for our benefit."

"I know the location of one of these meeting places," Novius revealed to Hilarion's surprise. "A meeting was held there today, and on the seventh day there will be another. But I must be protected in this matter."

"What do you mean?"

"My wife is one of them. I just found it out today."

"Your wish is to arrest all but her?"

"My wish is for an immediate divorce," Novius answered with vehemence, all his anger against his wife's imagined lover being transferred to this superstitious cult which he felt had stifled her capacity for love. "I will arrange to have the soldiers led to the meeting place. Order them to arrest those assembled at once without their teacher. They will then be vulnerable and easily influenced. As for me, I want only two things. Keep the arrest quiet until she is no longer my wife, and let me be the one to take the word to the emperor."

The day after this plan was carried out Saturus had been brought in to him at the praetorium, and Novius had talked with the priest at great length trying to discover what had attracted Perpetua to Christianity. It was true the man was possessed of an undeniable magnetism and a sincere and generous eloquence. When he spoke of the proofs of the existence of a supreme being, his exposition was logical and convincing. But this Jesus Christ, their leader! How could anyone conceive of him as a god? He'd sooner pay lip service to the deification of the emperors. They at least had one aspect of divinity — they had power and they knew enough to use it. But this tortured, ridiculed, bloody, naked figure hanging upon a cross — what godliness was there in him?

Saturus tried to gloss over the brutal facts with the fiction of a resurrection — that same old tired myth that mature educated men had long ago laid aside with their rattles and war clubs. How in the world could Perpetua have been taken in by that kind of irrational nonsense? The delusion wasn't so bad, but what it led to! For she had become incapable of honest human emotion. She was infatuated with a phantom, a shadow, a ghost. How could he fight against such a rival?

114

But he must put her from his mind, even as he had put her from his life. After the directive had come from the emperor, he had moved at once, driven to explosive action by smoldering resentment and forceful passions restricted by the staleness of his life. He had acted swiftly and irrevocably, or he might never have acted at all. Perhaps he had been cruel to allow her to be arrested, but she had used him cruelly too, in her own way, with her righteous disdain.

And it was not as if she were in any real danger. Her attachment to her baby at least was real and deep and strong, so strong that he was sure nothing could induce her to separate herself from him. Actually, he was doing her a good turn — he smiled to himself, in good spirits again — to shock her out of this unnatural religion before she became totally dehumanized.

The ship was rounding the point now and heading northward. Novius turned toward Marius again and clapped him on the shoulder. "This will be a great voyage," he said, and turning their backs on Carthage they strode forward to watch the ship cleave the wide expanse of water separating them from Rome.

MARK was so relieved when he left the prisoners to see that Felicity was somewhat recovered that he spoke to the jailer pleasantly and gave him forty denarii to see that wine and proper food was brought to the two sick prisoners. Thus conciliated, the jailer gave permission for Perpetua to have her baby with her, since as Mark explained he could hardly live apart from his mother at this time.

"She should have thought of that before," the jailer grumbled. "What will he do if she is condemned?" But he consented nevertheless.

Now as Mark rode home on his errand the wind on his face and the swift motion seemed to sweep his mind clear. He was thankful that he had been able to see Felicity; first because he felt that he had been able to do something to help her, but most of all because the sight of her had quieted the turmoil in his mind. The guilt of his love he now saw existed only in his own anguished conscience. To love was not wrong, but only to love wrongfully. He did love her — so much, so much! — but no longer with bitterness or jealousy, only with an ache and a sorrow so great that he knew nothing could release him from it but death.

116

The road to Megara lay through the cemeteries that ringed the city, confining the populous present within the bony band of its populous past. There were no trees along the road and only a few ancient olives could be seen in the distance bent and brooding over the rows of flat stones. The graves pressed close against the road as if jealous of even the smallest passageway left to the living. No one was in sight for it was still early afternoon, and the blinding glare of the sun on Mark's forehead made him suddenly aware that he was pressing his horse dangerously hard for this heat.

Since there was no place for man or beast to rest, he pulled up his horse and, dismounting, began to walk slowly close to the edge of the road taking advantage of the small squares and spears of shade from the tall steles and occasional mausoleums. The monuments increased in size and importance as they neared the road since high prices had to be paid for the privilege of declaiming the virtues of the deceased to every passerby. Mark walked by unseeing, dizzy, and weak, now that he was on foot, from the sun and lack of food and the two sleepless nights. A ring of pain tightened about his head and his throat became increasingly parched for he had had nothing to drink since early morning. The flat and desolate bleakness about him and his complete physical and mental exhaustion brought him to an overwhelming longing for suffering and death. If only he could be found worthy to suffer and die with Felicity! Yet how hard and bitter he knew his thoughts had been in the past two days! How fearfully self-willed and unresigned and desperate he had felt up until an hour ago when he had been calmed by her presence! Filled with remorse he dropped the reins of the horse in the shadow of a large mausoleum and walking ahead into the furnace of sunlight he fell to his knees on the sharp stones of the roadside.

Burn, burn, burn — was the plea from the depths of his heart. Burn, O God, all this hardness and dross from my soul that I may be purged and purified and made worthy to come at last to the trial to death!

Immobile in the blazing sunlight, on fire within with love and longing, he lost all awareness of his surroundings, of the sensations of his own body, of time, thought, or words — a small, silent, living torch among the silent stones.

How long he knelt there he had no knowledge, but he was roused by a cool rain upon his head and a grayness that blocked out the heat of the sun. He raised his head and let the rain fall onto his parched lips and into his mouth and onto his fevered face. Then he heard the excited joyful whinny of his horse, and he raised himself with new strength and mounting his horse, climbed out of the city's rim of the dead to the verdant hills of his home.

In sudden contrast were the green trees and grass, the many houses facing the road, the bright splotches of flowers revealed in the gardens. The rain had broken the silence and now chattered with busy cheerfulness on the roofs and the road. Here and there children dashed out with shouts and laughter to splash in the puddles and lift their faces to the refreshment from the skies. It was only with a firm hand that Mark restrained his horse's high spirits to a walk, if it could be called a walk, for even though the gait was slow it had a lilt in it, an impatient little side step that made it more of a dance than a walk. But Mark would not be hurried. He felt so restored in spirit and refreshed in body that he wished to savor every sight and

118

sound and texture of his homeland. He gazed about him with the gladness and intensity of a traveler returning home after a long absence, mingled with the fierce poignancy of one who must leave it soon forever.

All too soon came the last of this westward journey where the road cut off to the south and then doubled back to the city on a parallel route. Here was the little lane that climbed gradually between the orchards of the Villa Vivia and the walled gardens of Hasrafin, their only neighbor, to the heights on which both homes were built.

Mark smiled to himself now as he recalled a boyish escapade of his, when he had climbed that wall to pilfer two shining golden lemons from the carefully tended garden. Mark had been about ten at the time and, proud of his accomplishment, had boldly displayed his trophies at home. Old Hasrafin had been a very churlish neighbor, a surly Carthaginian who hated all things Roman with unquenchable bitterness. Never had he answered Aelianus with anything other than sarcastic gibes at the inefficiency and poor quality of his farming, with the result that at the Villa Vivia he became the target of many a verbal pleasantry. Mark remembered how tempting the strange and beautiful golden fruit had looked to him from the other side of the wall, and how he had reflected that to seize some of it from this crusty old Carthaginian would be a noble deed, worthy of a modern Scipio.

But when he related his feat with, he thought, the same witticism his elders used toward the old man, his father had quickly stripped off the glory and exposed him as a petty thief. Yet he was grateful to his father for his gentleness to him at that time, for recognizing that his own attitude had encouraged the boy's prank. Aelianus had himself gone with Mark and the lemons to make his apologies to Hasrafin. Even at the time Mark admired the tact with which his father spoke to the dour old curmudgeon, and now as he looked back he realized that the same qualities of honesty and diplomacy he showed then must have been a big factor in his father's earlier political success. Strangely enough, from that time on the relations between the neighbors ameliorated, and Aelianus put aside his pride enough to ask for advice in his farming, and Hasrafin, mollified by the Roman's humility, did indeed give him many helpful tips and an occasional slip from a rare plant. Each year at Saturnalia he sent over a basket of lemons labeled especially for Mark.

Mark could smell the lemons now, sharp and pungent, and mingled with them the wild and welcome tang of the sea. How he loved this spot where he had lived so much of his life, where he had been so close to the earth, where he had renewed over and over, by the sea, on the land, his love of God, his thankfulness, his trust! He felt now that he had regained the peace of mind that had sustained him during the years he had striven to fulfill his obligations as a son while preparing for his total dedication to God.

This then is what I have prepared for, he thought, this final holocaust. The love I have felt for Felicity was not to distract me but rather to intensify my dedication, that all my energies — my heart, my feelings, as well as my will and my mind — should come to culmination in this last complete renunciation in the arena.

XVI

Two weeks passed. Secundulus had never recovered from his fever and was now revered as the first martyr. The prisoners had been moved to another part of the prison that was drier and lighter and, thanks to regular offerings from the Christian community, were given adequate food and bedding.

Perpetua had her baby with her, and Felicity was amazed to see how happy she was. She was gayer and brighter than she had been in a long time. She played with Publius and laughed and sang to him as if she were in a palace instead of a prison. Her happiness was truly genuine. After her first shock and horror when she faced the possibility of her husband's complicity in their arrest, she had felt a profound relief. Freed from any need for loyalty to him, she was released from the tension of her conflicting emotions. It no longer mattered, she thought, recalling her vision, what he held in his hand, whether he offered her love or hate, he was only trying to drag her down — away from her total absorption in God. But he could not reach her any more; she had escaped his hands. He had no power any longer even to puzzle or disturb her. She could forgive him his desertion, even his plotting, if he were guilty, because by those actions he had set her free — free to turn her thoughts completely to God and to the moment of her final triumph.

Even her joy in her baby was colored by this thought, for with prudence she began to prepare him for their separation. With great patience she began to teach him to eat, mashing the finest parts of her food and mixing it to a thin consistency with water. At first he took it as a new game and bounced and jumped on her knee and stretched out for the dish until half of it spilled on the floor. The food was too precious to waste in that way, so finally Felicity had to hold him and keep his hands down so that Perpetua could get him to eat. But after a while he grew accustomed to his new diet and demanded less and less of his mother.

They had a large gourd to drink from and when Perpetua tried to teach Publius to drink from it the baby would reach for it and end by spilling everything. The jailer, noticing the attempt of the baby to take hold of the big gourd, brought him a small one with a handle just right for him to hold. This was the boy's only possession. He learned to drink from it, he played with it, crawled about with it in his hands, and went to sleep with it. No one could get it away from him. His mother could not even touch it to steady him when he drank.

Perpetua didn't have enough clothes to keep the baby swaddled, so they let him crawl about naked. Every morning, using their veils for rags, they scrubbed the floor of the little cell clean for the baby. He soon learned to pull himself up at the stool or the door and even took a few steps around the sides of the cell. His newfound freedom was a delight, and his laughter echoed and reechoed against the stones.

Perpetua's joy in the baby and her matter-of-fact acceptance of their fate made it easier for Felicity to retain the composure — almost contentment — that she had experienced after they had been brought here. She put her forebodings from her mind and felt secure for the time in God's protection.

The jailer, who was named Pudens, had been the object of an intense campaign for conversion on the part of Saturus. More than a little convinced by the priest and impressed by the courage and cheerfulness of the women, he began to show them any kindness which was in his power to grant them. The greatest favor was his permission for the men and women to spend the mornings together.

These meetings were of the utmost comfort to Revocatus. He needed Felicity so much. In the long days that followed in dull succession after he had laid her down upon the pallet in her cell and had then been herded into another cell away from her, he seemed to lose all faith.

Saturus, knowing that Revocatus had had the least instruction of them all, spent much time talking to him, retelling the story of Jesus and explaining his teachings in a simple way. But Revocatus had not come to God through words, and words could not reach him now. He did not question the willingness of the others to suffer for their faith, but he did not comprehend it. He never doubted that he himself would suffer courageously with them, but he saw it all as meaningless and pitiable. It was as if he had been drawn to God by the slender thread of Felicity's love and he had lost hold of the end. He knew it was still there, but it was hanging in a void and he could not reach it.

When they were at last allowed to visit, he was surprised to see Felicity looking so well, since he had not seen her conscious after she had collapsed on the march. He touched her hand only, conscious of the presence of the others, and said very low, "I have been so worried about you, Felicity. You have suffered so much, and I can do nothing for you."

"I do not suffer any more, Revocatus. I feel quite changed. I was so near to death. It was almost as if I had died and been brought back to life, and it does not seem so frightening to die. Now I know that God is with me. And really and truly, I don't suffer any more."

These words depressed Revocatus all the more, because now he felt that she would die and go off where he could never hope to follow. She seemed so remote. Life he knew, and evil, and suffering — but this God, this future life — how could he share it? For he was not so blind as to think he could reach God by being mangled by a lion unless he had come to him first.

"Oh, Felicity," he said hopelessly, "what am I to do? I can't believe in God — I can't even hope. You are my only goodness — you are my God."

"No, don't say that," and she took him away as far as she could from the others. She was not shocked by his words, because she knew he did not mean them the way they sounded, but she did not want anyone else to hear. His simplicity and his humility were so great, and it made her love him more because of his weakness and his need.

"You do know God, Revocatus," she assured him. "The goodness in me that you love — that is from God. The

124

goodness in you that I love — that is from God too. No, don't deny it. I know the goodness in you. Why do you think I love you? Can you doubt that I love you?

"And there is a greater goodness that you and I know when we are together. It is something outside of us that neither you nor I have alone. We cannot lose it without losing our love completely. That goodness is the goodness of God.

"What will it be to die?" Felicity groped for a better understanding in the need to explain it to Revocatus. "Surely it will be to know better that love of God that we already have a share in. Do you remember that you said that one minute of our love was worth your whole lifetime? To die will be to see that one minute made eternal, with all the accidents of time and the world dropping away. Life and death swirl around us but we hold the string on which they are tethered, and we will stand in the center of existence, in our love and in the love of God."

Revocatus could not understand her words, but to hold her hand and feel her love and trust was enough for him, and he was content to accept from her the faith he could not himself comprehend.

XVII

FOR a while after Secundulus died, Saturninus was quiet and morose, so much so that Saturus chided him on one occasion for grieving too much, in that his father had been called by God and had in fact been spared much suffering.

"I know that is true, Father," Saturninus said a little impatiently, "but do I love God any the less because I sorrow for my father? He was not only my father, but my partner. We shared all our labors these past twenty years. He fired the ovens and did all the castings and helped me with those wretched pots. I'm not ashamed to grieve for him as I hope my wife will grieve for me. But she will weep and that will make it easier. I cannot weep."

However, Saturninus realized the rebuke was kindly meant, and it was then he spoke to Pudens and received the second favor from the jailer. The next morning Pudens brought in a large lump of common clay. It was hard and dried out, but Saturninus declared it was just what he wanted. Pudens also found him a wobbly table which Saturninus made steady on the stone floor by placing his blanket underneath the legs. With these preparations he went to work and the loneliness and sorrow in him worked its way out through the steady movements of his large muscular hands.

For two whole days he worked the clay with his fingers, moistening it ever so slightly, but mostly softening it by working it with his hands until the warmth and body oils made it pliable. Every inch of the clay was separately manipulated and then worked back into the mass. The prisoners watched him with interest — there was little else to do — curious to see the amount of patient preparation he put into simply the texture of the stuff.

Finally he was satisfied that it was smooth and soft, and he took about a third of the clay and molded it into a base that looked as rough and craggy as the piece had been to begin with. Above this mass he now fashioned a straight narrow smooth column about a foot and a half tall that seemed to rise from and out of the lumpy clay. Saturninus spent a whole day finishing and shaping this column and when he was through one would almost think that the rough base and the smooth shaft had been constructed out of two different materials so greatly did they differ in texture.

He had only a sharp stick and a knife to work with beside his fingers, but now it was the matter of only an hour to strip away the exterior of the column and uncover the pattern that had been in his mind. It was the figure of a woman rising on one knee, bent over as with sorrow and grief, but pulling herself upward from the rough clay below. The figure was beautiful in its rounded curves so perfectly shaped from the straight tall column. One could still see the column in the figure, tall and precious, like a shaft of marble. Even though the figure itself was bent over, it gave the impression of upward movement, of striving, of reaching.

Saturninus worked in silence and the others watched in

silence, in wonder at the dexterity that made the hard clay appear soft as flesh and gave the stiff dead stuff the feeling of movement. But now the sculptor stopped, and when he glanced up his eyes met those of the priest. He smiled a little half smile and said apologetically, "What a poor sort of Christian I am! I grieve for my father. I can't stop making statues. Let's hope I do a better job of dying."

But Saturus did not smile. He was struck by the instinctive wordless response of all to the beauty and the feeling in the statue, and he was humbled before a man's soul exposed in a work of his own creation. For once, words did not come easily as he struggled to express an idea completely new to him.

"I didn't understand, Saturninus, believe me, I didn't understand. All I saw before were the idols, the pagan gods and goddesses, and I didn't look beyond them. I had no idea of what you put into your work, and of what you could give us. For that talent should have been used instead of suppressed."

Saturus recalled the brusqueness with which he had told the sculptor to destroy his statues — gods and goddesses, yes, in name, but in reality the perfection of humanity as he had seen it. He thought of the hunger for creation that he had stifled without a second thought, so full was he of his own virtue, so confident in his own judgment. It had been pride, he admitted, pride in his own eloquence that had made him disdain this other ability. Words cannot say everything, nor can everyone understand them, but this statue spoke from soul to soul directly. The beauty and nobility of man, in his suffering and his sorrow, striving ever upward — humanity itself — not in a thousand words could he express what this sculptor had revealed in clay. It was at the same time a vision and a prayer.

"I was at fault," he confessed, "not to recognize this human need — of yours, to create, and of ours, to respond. You have come out better than I have in this matter, Saturninus. If you die as well as you work, I envy you."

XVIII

HILARION prepared carefully for the day of trial for the Christians. He had a large platform constructed in the forum with a raised canopied chair for himself as judge and at his right an altar for sacrifice. This work caused much talk and inquiry, as he had intended, and it was not long until everyone in Carthage knew that there would be an interrogation of Christians on the ninth day of September at midday. This time was chosen because the son of Septimius Severus, who had recently been given the title of Caesar, was celebrating his birthday on the fifteenth day. Hilarion wished to have everything in readiness for a wild beast and gladiatorial show in the amphitheater in honor of the new Caesar.

In order to make sure that he had a receptive audience for the inquiry, Hilarion called in a certain Saprino, a fellow that lived on the wharves whom the governor found useful as a contact man and a source of information. This former stevedore had been caught stealing from members of his own crew and they had taken their own means of justice by cutting off both his hands. He stole no more nor did he work, but he was tolerated now by the others for they knew he had the ear of the governor. Whenever Hilarion wished a cheering throng to impress visiting dignitaries or to direct the minds of the people, Saprino was always able to recruit a large if somewhat unruly crowd.

The prisoners were not told of the time of their interrogation though rumors had reached them that it would be soon. Yet when they were interrupted in the middle of their noon meal and roughly hustled out into the streets so jammed with people that the soldiers had to force a way with their spears, it was with a shock that they left the prison which seemed now like a sanctuary.

A large crowd followed the prisoners all the way from the prison to the forum, but the wiser ones had gone to the forum earlier and made sure of vantage points on the steps of the temples of Diana and Aesculapeius or in the embrasures of the windows of the public buildings. A few daring individuals had climbed to the roofs and sat upon the ridge poles dangling their feet over the carved friezes. Totally disregarding the commands of the priests to descend, they hooted and made derisive gestures at the military police who attempted to enforce the requests until at last they were ignored and left in undisputed possession of their precarious box seats.

It was not until the prisoners were at the foot of the scaffold that the governor made his entrance, and took his place on the magisterial chair with the imperial eagle at his right side and the standard of the Third Augustan legion at his left. When the crowd was silenced, Hilarion rose and explained the purpose of the assembly in a carefully prepared and delivered speech. He was an able orator and the hired claqueurs insured that applause was forthcoming at the proper places.

"It has been brought to our attention, my dear people, by our noble and illustrious emperor, Septimius Severus [*loud applause*], whose unparalleled victories in Parthia have brought further renown on the glorious Roman empire [*loud applause*], and whose career is regarded with the greatest pride by all in this province of Africa, since he is the noblest of all Africa's sons [*loud and continuous applause*], so noble indeed that he is ranked among the gods [*more applause*] — he it is who has brought to our attention an ugly evil that is recurring throughout the empire and which must be stamped out at once without mercy. This is that treasonous sect called Christians who are guilty of every crime, even the most abominable of all, the eating of human flesh.

"Furthermore, the one simple act which we ask as a token of allegiance to Rome, they refuse to do, to make sacrifice to Jupiter for the health and safety of our glorious emperor and for the protection of our country.

"Make no mistake about it, my countrymen. Let not your human pity overcome you. These Christians, though seemingly innocent and mild in appearance, are capable of the grossest, most infamous, and most inhuman crimes.

"But know and understand, my friends and you prisoners also, that the mercy of the divine Severus is as great as his power. Regardless of what you have done in the past, you that are accused before me, you have only to come forward willingly and offer sacrifice for the honor and glory of the emperor and you will go free. Refuse and you will be condemned to fight the beasts in the arena.

"Lictor, bring forward the prisoners."

There was an angry growling outcry from the crowd as the three men were brought up the steps of the platform and made to stand before the proconsul. Hilarion's secretary,

132

who stood beside him, briefed him on the persons before him, for Hilarion prided himself on using no notes. There was a delay now, and Hilarion could see that an old man had hold of one of the women and was talking with her, attempting to keep her from climbing the steps. He motioned to the lictor who struck the old man on the chest with his rod, forcing him to give way and allowing the two women to mount the platform.

"That was M. Vivius Aelianus," whispered the secretary, "a friend of Minucius, very anti-Christian. It is his daughter who is accused."

Hilarion did not know the old man, but he knew Perpetua. He had met her once in company with Novius. When the women appeared on the platform, a surprised murmur went through the crowd for they seemed so young and pitiable.

Hilarion turned to them first and spoke kindly and gently, mindful of his friendship with Novius and in fact stirred with pity himself.

"Prisoners, remember, the choice is yours. You have only to take the incense and place it on the fire of this altar and pray for the welfare of the emperor and you may leave and rejoin your family and friends. Refuse and you face death."

Perpetua stood with dignity and pride and made no move toward the altar. When she spoke, her voice was as clear and ringing as the governor's and carried throughout the entire forum which was still and hushed before this living drama.

"Never will I sacrifice to these false gods. There is but one God and his son is Jesus Christ whom you also killed. Him only do I worship. Threats and torture and death can never turn me from my faith. And I warn you, Hilarion, yes, and I warn you too, Septimius Severus, that unless you turn from these false gods and worship the one true God, he will destroy both you and Rome with you!"

Now the crowd became wild, shouting for death and pressing close to the platform. Rocks were thrown until Hilarion held up his hand to restore order.

"Sentence will be pronounced after all the prisoners have been interrogated. If the people are not quiet, the prisoners will be removed and the questioning held privately."

This effectively silenced the crowd since everyone wished to see the whole of the trial. Now Hilarion questioned Felicity, Revocatus, and Saturninus in turn and they each in a low voice refused to sacrifice. Saturus, who had been the first on the platform, was the last one questioned by Hilarion.

He stepped forward toward the altar and prayed in a clear and resonant voice that filled the whole of the hushed forum.

"O God, we humbly pray you to bless our emperor. Guide him that he may rule this empire with justice and wisdom. We ask for him a long life, undisturbed power, security at home, brave armies, a faithful senate, an upright people, and a peaceful world!"

The people were silent, not really understanding whether Saturus was following the directive of the proconsul or not, since the term *deus* was used for Jupiter. Even Hilarion was startled at the words.

"Will you then sacrifice to Jupiter?" he questioned again.

"When you sacrifice to Jupiter," Saturus went on, "it is good and proper. For you worship the power of God under this name, and God recognizes this humility and this desire as a true sacrifice.

"But for me to sacrifice to Jupiter is a mockery. It is a

mockery to you who sincerely worship God even in this imperfect manner. It is a mockery to God since I know the one true God and the one true sacrifice — the sacrifice that Jesus Christ made on the cross and now renews on our altars. This is the only sacrifice which I can make, this and the sacrifice of my own life."

Hilarion turned on Saturus, angry that he had tricked them all into listening to him so intently. He had had a more attentive audience than Hilarion himself.

"If you are not going to sacrifice," he thundered, "be silent and prepare to die!"

Now Hilarion's hired group recognized the place for shouts, for during Saturus' speech they had been confused and disturbed. The whole crowd took up the word too and reiterated "Die! Die!" but when Saturus spoke again they fell silent, for he had stirred their curiosity and their wonder.

"If you forbid me to speak, my blood will cry out. You will truly sow the dragon's teeth, for where each one of us falls, a hundred more will rise to take our place!"

"Enough!" shouted Hilarion. "For this obdurance forty lashes will be administered to the prisoners now, and, Lictor, start with this man!"

It seemed then as if the whole forum burst into wild applause, thirsting and howling for this punishment, yet if one looked more closely one could see that where two men were shouting one was standing thoughtful and silent, and so throughout the assembly about one third of those present, unnoticed in the turmoil, were still.

One togaed Roman pushed his way through the crowd and mounted the lower steps of the platform to stand just below the proconsul where he was visible to all, yet in an attitude of suppliance.

135

"Worthy proconsul," he addressed Hilarion, "will you grant me permission to speak?"

The secretary whispered to the proconsul, "The brother of Perpetua." Hilarion nodded permission. "Speak."

"I know that Your Excellency is aware of the law forbidding the execution of a mother who is with child. I believe you have a situation of this kind here."

"You are right, sir, and you are also right in thinking that I know this law." Hilarion was crisp and abrupt. "Sentence has not been pronounced. You will see that the sentence in this one case will be delayed until the law has the authority to complete its execution."

"I believe you will find that this same law applies not only to execution but also to cases of extreme corporal punishment," Mark continued, "since this endangers the life of the unborn child. There was a case, of which I have the record, under Marcus Aurelius, in which both a lictor and the official authorizing the punishment were convicted of murder because of stillbirth brought on by such a punishment."

Hilarion hesitated only a few moments before replying. "Obviously you misunderstood the order." He repeated it now so that the lictor too would understand it clearly. "The order of forty lashes applies to the male prisoners only. But" — for he had had too much from Perpetua and her family — "ten lashes will be given to the female prisoners — on the face." Now he warmed to the subject. "It would indeed be unkind for us to pronounce sentence of death on these two young women who do not understand what pain really is and what a terrible choice they are making. Surely in all charity we should make an attempt to dissuade them in yet another way. By this lesser chastisement we can yet hope to waken them to their extreme peril and guide them from the jaws of bloody death."

The cries of "Hear! Hear!" on all sides reassured Hilarion that he had turned this exchange to his advantage. Yet Mark had made his point also, and the lictor was extremely cautious in administering the lashes to Felicity and the proconsul took no official notice of the lightness of the strokes.

Hilarion turned privately to his secretary. "Have that man brought to my house for questioning, not by soldiers. Just send a request that he await me there."

So it was that after the sentence had been pronounced and the prisoners removed, a slave approached Mark and asked him to follow him to the governor's house. He had no time to see his parents, for he had been separated from them after he addressed the governor, but he left with a great surge of gladness. He had seen the proconsul's anger at the momentary discomfiture he had caused him, and he was sure now that he would be granted that gift of martyrdom for which he longed.

At the governor's house he was shown into a small office where he was left alone for several hours while the proconsul made his return from the forum, dined, and took his rest. The time did not seem long to Mark, however, for he was elated by the thought that his declaration was at hand. He rehearsed to himself what he would say when the proconsul questioned him and prepared long rhetorical speeches after the manner of Saturus. None of them sounded quite right as he practiced them in whispers, and he finally decided on the simple answer,

"Yes, I am a Christian. I believe in the one true God and his son Jesus Christ who died on the cross for us. For this faith I will gladly lay down my life."

Hilarion came in, walking quickly, and took Mark completely off balance by apologizing for his delay. "I'm sorry I kept you so long." He sat down and motioned Mark to a chair. "Thank you for waiting."

Mark sat down, for he could not very well refuse and murmured that it was no matter. Then Hilarion began to talk with him very pleasantly and courteously, asking questions about his family, especially about his father, and about his home and the estates from which they derived their livelihood.

Finally Hilarion turned to him abruptly and said, "You do not ask for mercy for your sister?"

"No," Mark declared and waited tensely for the next question.

Hilarion looked at him for what seemed an eternity, silently, with a strange smile on his lips. Then he rose and dismissed him. "You may go." It was at once a permission and a command.

"I am free to go?" Mark asked in astonishment.

"You may go," Hilarion repeated and waited for his departure. Novius had been right, recalled the proconsul, these bloody executions accomplish nothing. This man before him had been so charged with zeal after the spectacle this afternoon that he was eager to leap into death. Hilarion wondered a bit why he had not declared himself at once. Perhaps in spite of his zeal he had not the courage of his sister. She had plenty, there was no doubt about that, enough for the whole family. But this was surely not the way to handle the problem. The execution of these five he was committed to because of their accursed stubbornness, but he would create no more heroes.

There were other methods — more devious and more

profitable. This family now had very attractive holdings at the farthest part of the Cape where he had always wished to have a summer home. The father and present master was well known to be virulently anti-Christian, so he could not proceed against him. But he had certainly looked old today at the trial. This shock would, Hilarion hoped, bring him soon to his grave.

If something happened to the old man and his son became the master, then, ah then, this young man would find out how he liked being made not a hero, but a beggar!

MARK made his way from the proconsul's house in a daze. Ever since his first despair over Felicity's arrest, he had been bouyed up by action, by consistently jeopardizing himself, until the moment of climax this afternoon which he had been sure would bring about his own arrest. Should he have declared himself and insisted upon being arrested? No, he felt, the decision was not his to make. If God had only thought him worthy. . . .

He felt himself slipping back into that same despair. No, no, no, he must not make that mistake again. Worthy or not, God would do with him as he chose. It was not for him to question the decision, but to accept it and to meet it and to act upon it. Surely he could live with as much courage as he had thought to die.

Thus determined, he made his way to Crispus' house, where he mounted his horse and rode toward home. As he rode he came to the conclusion that he could now no longer doubt that he was meant to be a priest. His way was clear. His mother and Gaius were obviously as safe from persecution as he was, and there was nothing to keep him from leaving his home at once and being ordained as soon as possible.

It would be better for him not to stay here. He knew his

own weakness. He would gladly have suffered with her, but he could not watch.

He would go to Hippo tomorrow. The bishop might decide that in the emergency his education was complete enough and ordain him immediately. Then when Saturus fell, even at that moment his prophecy would begin to come true. There would be a priest to take his place.

He spurred his horse on, anxious to tell his mother of his safety and of his determination, his renewed dedication.

*   *   *

But when he arrived at home, he did not tell it. He could see the house from a distance for every room was lighted. His father must be mourning Perpetua as already dead, he thought, and he was in a haste to tell his father and mother of his own safe return. When he entered the atrium no one was there, there were no signs of formal mourning. He could see that the lamps had been carelessly placed and imperfectly lighted for the wicks were not trimmed properly and the light was alternately sputtering and flaring up.

"Mother!" he called out, with a kind of dread, for this unusual display of light meant some evil the slaves were trying to ward off. "It is I, Mark. Where are you?"

"Mark, Mark!" she called back from an inner room, and her voice was so broken and choked that he could hardly recognize it. They met at the entrance from the atrium and she fell into his arms with incoherent weeping and the constant reiteration of his name, as if she were trying to convince herself of his presence.

"Mother, Mother, do not weep so." He had never seen her so beside herself, and thinking the distress was for him, he reassured her, "I am all right. Can I speak freely? Where is Father?"

"It doesn't matter." She spoke numbly now, without emotion. "Speak what you will. Nothing matters now. . . . He cannot hear, but he knows anyway."

"Is he dead then?"

"No, he lives and breathes, but cannot move or speak or hear. It happened after we came home from the trial. Gaius was here before us waiting in front of the door in a state of great excitement. He said that you, too, had been arrested.

"Then, without a pause, he declared that he too was a Christian and that he would no longer stay under this roof and be subject to the authority of one who consented to the murder of his brother and sister.

"'No longer,' he shouted at me, 'will I live a lie like you and Mark have been living all these years!'

"I guess he rode off then. I didn't notice, because your father looked at me and I couldn't say anything. But he knew, Mark, he knew. . . . And then it happened; he tried to speak, but he couldn't. He tried to take a step and then he fell forward, face down in the dust of the roadside." She covered her face in dry agony, and her whole body shook in a horrified trembling remembrance.

"Mother," Mark said, "don't worry. We will face this together. I will not leave you." No, he would not leave her — his father helpless, the child disowned and motherless, Perpetua on her way to death, Gaius gone — no, he would not leave her. God had his own way of showing his decision. He had been twice rejected — but there was still a course laid out for him that he must complete.

"There is no further danger," he reassured his mother. He had to speak slowly and plainly to calm her and to reach through her despair. "If Father knows that you and I are

Christian too, what of it? Can we act any differently now? Shall we love him the less because he is helpless?"

"It is my fault," she sobbed. "His children he could bear, but, when he looked at me, he could not forgive me — oh, I have loved him so."

"Love him now, even more," Mark urged.

"He rejects me. I can see it in his eyes. He doesn't want me around."

"I will see him." Mark led the way to Aelianus' room, which was smoky hot and bright with a lamp burning on every table. In the far corner stood the altar to the household gods. Aelianus was lying on his bed, so motionless that he seemed dead except for the recognition which lit his eyes as Mark drew near. With a terrible effort he raised his left hand a few inches off the bed and his face became dreadfully contorted as he tried to speak. Finally one sound burst out, a harsh inhuman squawk which only the ears of love could distinguish as Mark's name.

Mark fell to his knees at his bedside and took his father's hand, and all the tension and weariness and sorrow that he had held at bay all these weeks broke out at last in an uncontrolled and prolonged weeping. When finally his anguish was spent, he was suddenly conscious of the silence in the room. It was so still that the breathing of the paralyzed man sounded loud and heavy. His father's hand clung to Mark's with a strength that was surprising, like the grip of a drowning man on the line that could pull him to safety.

"Father," Mark said, speaking in a loud voice and forming the words exactly with his lips, "can you hear me?"

Understanding showed in Aelianus' face, and he made that terrible tortured grimace again trying to speak, but Mark pressed his left hand with his.

143

"Do not try to speak, Father. I will tell you what happened." He continued speaking very slowly in a loud voice, watching his father all the time to make sure he understood.

"The proconsul kept me waiting a long time, but then he just talked to me. I don't know what he wanted. He asked me about you and the estates and about the income from them. Then suddenly he asked, 'Do you not ask mercy for your sister?' I said 'No,' and he seemed to be waiting for something. Then all of a sudden he sent me away."

Aelianus was trying to speak again and he rasped out a single incomprehensible syllable. But Mark guessed it at once, for in retelling the strange interview he suddenly saw what he had missed before.

"A bribe!" he burst out. "That's what he was waiting for!" He had been so stupid, so engrossed in his own thoughts during the interview that he had missed the point of the proconsul's question entirely.

But now with a tremendous effort Aelianus pressed Mark's hand so hard that he held it down and without trying to speak at all conveyed his meaning exactly.

"No," Mark interpreted. "No, I will not offer him a bribe. Perpetua would not want it either. She would prefer to die with the others."

Mark was silent then, only holding his father's hand, for he could feel his anguished helplessness, the bereavement, and sorrow, and even more the fear sealed up in his imprisoned body. His father had always been so strong, so decisive, so thoroughly in command of his household, and Mark could read his fear that now that he was helpless, his children, his wife, whom he knew to be Christian, would act completely contrary to his wishes. It showed in the matter of the bribe. Mark thought it unwise to refer in any way to

144

Christianity or to his father's knowledge of his faith, but he had to find a way to let him know that his own filial devotion was unchanged.

"Father, I swear to you," he said solemnly, "that I will not disregard your wishes in this or in any other matter. I will not abandon you. You are my father and the head of this house. By all that is holy to both of us I pledge you all my devotion and service." The words were simple and no one, least of all Mark, thought them reckless or even touched with courage.

Aelianus relaxed and seemed satisfied. He closed his eyes and his breathing became more regular so that Mark thought that he slept. Mark did not let go of his hand, though it now lay limp in his. Suddenly his father's eyes flew open and the pressure on Mark's hand became a hard and terrible pleading.

"What is it, Father?" Mark asked. "Do not try to speak. Do you want food? Wine?"

But the pressure on his hand denied these and still the eyes pleaded. Then they turned from Mark to another object in the room and back again begging him to follow. Mark had to turn half around to see where they led.

It was to the altar of the household gods.

Every night of his life Aelianus prayed to the household gods that he had carried with him when he fled from Rome. Every night he made a prayer of thanksgiving and of petition at this altar and then placed incense on the lamp kept burning before it. The father was the high priest of the family and nothing was asked of the household except their presence. Since it was unavoidable in a pagan household, mere attendance at these rites was not forbidden to Christians.

From earliest days these nightly prayers had been familiar to Mark. There was a quiet and peace about the ritual that had been impressive even when he was squirming and restive in his childhood and anxious to be gone. Most of the time the prayers were short and formal, but in times of anxiety or stress the prayers were often of great length.

After Mark had become a Christian he always prayed to God silently at these times begging mercy for this error and asking blessings on his family and guidance for himself. Then in some way he sensed a bond of unity in the family even though he knew in his mind it did not exist.

Mark knew his father's meaning at once. In the absence or illness of the father, no slave, no woman could make the offering in his stead. Only his son.

But this was too much! When he had pledged his service to his father he had not promised that!

Well, Mark calmed himself, there was no need to break his promise. How could he be expected to know what this speechless man wanted? No one else could begin to understand him. Even his mother thought of him as one dead. Now that his father was without speech or movement, now was the time to put aside these pagan practices and live his faith openly.

"I don't understand what you want, Father," he lied. He had always been a poor liar, and the shock of his face revealed it now, and the way he turned his eyes away. His father knew it to be a lie, and he knew that his father knew it.

But then Mark was angry with himself for caring if his father knew. And he aroused himself to anger at his father also, thinking, "It is a test. He is challenging me, even as the proconsul challenged Perpetua." He raised his head in

146

defiance to face his father. But when he met his father's eyes he saw in them not a challenge but only a great helpless pleading. How could this paralyzed man challenge him when he had no force or power or even words left to him, and in fact lay there completely at his mercy?

But how could his father ask this of him? Was this not what Perpetua was in prison and about to die for? The true and right worship of God. How could he be a party to pagan rites? Not all the pity in the world could move him to do this thing.

"No, no, no!" he shouted, and his mother wondered at the vehemence and intensity of this one-sided conversation. "Never will I do it!"

All this time Aelianus had been gripping Mark's hand with an unremitting fierceness while he sought with all the power in his eyes to hold him to the pledge he had so solemnly spoken. But now at Mark's savage declaration his hand grew limp and his eyes became glazed with a blank despair. Then he closed them and lay as still and hopeless as death itself.

He is a prisoner too, Mark thought, and about to die. He is sealed up more irrevocably than Perpetua, denied any contact with man and with God. I am his only link.

What was it Saturus had said? That even the worship of Jupiter was good, in its imperfect way the worship of God.

How long had his father to live at any rate? A day? Two days? Had he the right to deny him this worship in his death agony? Would he be any better than Hilarion denying to Perpetua the right to worship as she believed?

But how long had he to live? A day? A week? A month? A year? And every night to confront this problem anew, to wrestle with its shifting shape with diminished powers, to decide again . . . and again . . . and again. . . .

He was still kneeling beside the bed and he buried his face on his father's still form in an agony of spirit. His father lay unmoving, no longer asking, no longer hoping, accepting his decision in total withdrawal.

"Oh God, forgive me," Mark prayed and pressed the hand beneath him strongly to open the door into the old man's isolation.

Aelianus opened his eyes and looked questioningly at Mark's tortured face.

"I will be your hands," Mark pledged, and then he began to sob to see the great joy in his father's eyes. "I cannot say the words." His voice was so choked now that his father could not understand. With a great effort he controlled himself and spoke loud and distinctly. "Pray silently, Father. When you have finished your prayer close your eyes so I will know."

He stood up and turned to go to the altar. As he did, he touched his father's hand fleetingly in a shy and childish gesture, murmuring, "Pray — pray for me," but his head was turned and his father did not know he had spoken.

Mark stood not in front of the altar but to the right so that his father could see. After a long time the old man closed his eyes but opened them quickly to make sure the rest of the sacrifice was carried out.

From twenty-five years of watching, Mark was able to copy exactly the familiar movements of his father. He moved slowly and deliberately, opening the box containing the incense, placing the grains of incense on the fire, replacing the cover on the box. But when the smoke began to rise, he turned precipitously and fled — out of the room, away from the smell of the incense, out into the courtyard, out beyond the poplars, out to the very brink of the sea.

148

XX

Novius returned to the town house of Marius' family in Rome and flung off his toga. The upper part of his tunic was dripping with sweat and his hair was plastered to his wet forehead. The town house was empty except for three slaves left there for his service while the family fled the September heat for their villa on the sea. Even Marius himself had deserted his beloved Rome.

Comfort apparently meant nothing to the emperor. Whenever he was not on campaign he was in Rome and he kept a tight rein on the senators and the administration. Rome was still the capital of his empire and there was to be no doubt in anyone's mind that the supreme ruler was Septimius Severus.

The sweat that covered Novius was not from the heat, because it was only seven o'clock in the morning. He had just come from an hour-long interview with the emperor, and he felt as limp and bedraggled as an old tunic that has been washed and beaten on the rocks of the river. The report about the Christians had been just the starting point, and there was no subject having to do with Africa that the emperor had not questioned him about. He had fired questions at him as rapidly as they could speak and his knowl-

149

edge of the country was so extensive and his perception so quick that Novius had to be very exact in his replies. The whole interview was taken down by a secretary and that made him all the more nervous.

He felt he had done well on the military matters and could answer the questions crisply with hardly a moment's thought, but when Severus had turned to the relations between the large and small landowners and other matters pertaining to trade and agriculture, he had foundered and bogged down in generalities to the obvious impatience of the emperor. Well, a man couldn't know everything, could he? But now he realized that he should have used the years he had spent in Africa for more acute observation. It seemed, as he thought over the interview, that all he had displayed was the vast extent of his ignorance.

But now his bath was drawn and he peeled off his tunic. He didn't have much time to refresh himself since he was due back at the palace in an hour. The emperor was indefatigable. The games were today and still he had been up before dawn working. Well, Novius thought as he relaxed in the bath, he must not have made such a bad showing this morning or Severus would not have asked him to be a part of his personal retinue today. But he dreaded the day ahead of him. He felt that the others who had been with the emperor longer were mocking him behind his back. Well, let them mock. The emperor was the only one that mattered.

But was this what he had struggled and contrived so for? How he had wanted to be noticed by the emperor! Little had he realized how fortunate he had been in the comparative obscurity of his provincial assignment. There he had been a great and proud man; here, after a few more interviews like the one this morning, he was afraid he'd end up a gibbering idiot.

Oh, come on now, Novius, he growled at himself as he put on fresh clothes and waited for the slave to adjust his toga, you've got better stuff in you than that. All you've got to do is make sure Severus recognizes it. . .

The glare and the noise of the city hit him like a blow as he stepped out of the empty house. How Rome had changed in the past six years! He had had a wonderful time in Rome when he was twenty-one. It had taken him only ten months to run through his inheritance, but wild and glorious months they had been! How he had thrilled then to the splendor of the temples and the palace and the brilliance of the court life!

Was Rome this dirty then? He picked his way through the narrow streets of the Subura amid the jostling sweaty crowds and looked up at the crest of the Capitoline Hill where he could see the temples of Mars and Venus and the great temple of Jupiter the Thunderer built by Augustus. They were far enough in the clouds not to see this squalor. The huge, rambling palace of the Caesars that had appropriated the whole of the Palatine Hill could be plainly seen from here, and if anyone cared to look, this noisome slum could be seen from the palace. But doubtless no one ever looked.

He wondered where all his former companions were that had been so "dear" to him when he was spending his money so wildly. He probably wouldn't recognize any of them if he saw them. He couldn't even remember their names any more. He had always been alone, but never had he felt so lonely as in these crowds. In this whole great, teeming, frantic capital of the world there was no one who knew or

151

cared if Novius lived or died. What a desolate place for all its hollow grandeur!

Well, he might as well face it. It wasn't Rome that had changed. Rome was still the same — it was he who had changed. And it was not in Rome alone that no one cared. Nowhere in the wide world did anyone care what happened to Novius!

So much the better. He was responsible to nobody, only to himself. That's the way he had entered the army with nothing but his good name and his driving ambition. That was the way he had come to the emperor's court — but somehow the ambition didn't seem enough to satisfy him any more.

Well, he would make it satisfy him! If he could only get a good appointment from the emperor and get out of this place. Action — fighting — that was what he needed. He was becoming stale and soft to allow himself to be beset by these womanish feelings.

*　　*　　*

Novius was surprised to find himself enjoying the games from the emperor's bloc of seats in the Colosseum. The emperor was especially friendly to him and spoke to him as one soldier to another. The gladiatorial combats were far superior to anything he had seen in Carthage, and the combats between the equally armed swordsmen were real contests of skill. Novius began to relax and found himself discussing the gladiators and their techniques freely with the emperor. Swordsmanship he knew and here he felt on firm ground.

The emperor was in excellent spirits and the contests were so well fought that not once did he give the sign of condemnation to the vanquished gladiator. Perhaps that is

152

why the gladiators are better in Rome, Novius thought; in Carthage they never lived long enough to learn anything.

When the first contest between the retarius, a man without armor who had only a trident and a net for protection, and a gladiator began, Novius found himself completely uninterested. The two danced about, feinting at each other from a distance, posturing and shouting more like actors in a comedy than like combatants. Novius found that Severus was equally disgruntled and they amused themselves by joking and laughing at the obviously faked groans and dodges of the fighters.

"I believe they drew straws before they came out to see who'll take the fall," Novius hazarded. "I'll bet a sestercium it's the retarius."

He had not intended to address the bet to the emperor, but Severus took it up. "Done!" he cried. "I'll wager the gladiator falls."

Hardly had he spoken when the gladiator gained an advantage over his opponent and the retarius was on the ground with a sword at his throat, pleading for mercy. With hardly a glance Severus turned thumbs down and then signaled to the master of the games. "I don't like clowns in the arena," he said coldly. "Match that gladiator with Marimbo."

The triumphant gladiator was walking from the center of the arena with his bloody sword unsheathed when he was stopped and made to turn and face Marimbo, the greatest retarius of them all. Loud cheers went up from the crowd as the famed retarius in two swift movements disarmed the gladiator with his trident and rendered him helpless with the net. The gladiator now drew as short shrift from the emperor as had his former victim.

As the bodies were being dragged from the arena, Severus turned to Novius and his face was hard. "Now who wins the bet?" he challenged in Punic.

Novius managed a laugh. "Neither of those two, for a certainty," he replied in the same language. Thank god I learned Punic! he thought to himself.

"Well answered." Severus smiled, commending not his wit, but his accent, and then he continued speaking in Punic to Novius for some time, much to the annoyance of the others in the emperor's retinue for they understood not a word, and they were envious to see how delighted Severus was for this opportunity to speak his native tongue freely with another.

At last the emperor reverted to Latin to include the rest of the group. "Tell us," he said as the bouts proceeded, "what do you think of the Roman gladiators compared to the Carthaginians?"

"With the exception of those two so properly dispatched, sire, the ones at Rome are far superior," Novius answered. He was no longer at ease and chose his words with the greatest care.

"But the beasts," put in one of the courtiers, "surely the beasts are much better in Africa?"

"Far from it," Novius answered with a strained laugh. "The best are shipped here for the pleasure of the emperor, as is only right and proper. We are left with the old and the crippled that couldn't stand the trip by sea. I once saw a prisoner get the better of a lion with his bare hands. I doubt if the lion had any teeth at all, he was so feeble. It does make it a little more of a contest."

"The next event should be an interesting contest," the director of the games put in for the benefit of them all. "We

154

have by chance a perfect match. It is rare that entire families of beasts are captured in the wilds. Here we have a lioness and her cubs pitted against a mother and two sons."

"What is their crime?" Novius asked. He could see the three walking slowly out into the center of the arena, the mother holding her children close and slowing her steps to match their reluctant ones.

"They are Christians," Severus replied. "And mark how the mother is forcing her children to this horrible fate. This is the most revolting part of these fanatics and what makes them so dangerous. They are completely without any human feeling."

A courtier spoke up. "So many of them are slaves and in such wretched circumstances that they don't consider death an evil. Especially, I'm told, as they believe it is just the beginning of a new life."

"If death is what they want," Severus responded, "we can satisfy them. But watch now; you'll see in contrast what a much greater concern the lioness has for her young."

It was true, the lioness made sure each of the cubs had a carcass to gorge himself on before she settled down to her own feast.

Novius was sick and revolted as he sat speechless before this dreadful carnage. The woman was an Asiatic Jewess who did not look at all like Perpetua, yet it was his wife he saw standing in the arena and whom he was forced to watch overtaken by savage death.

The mother love he had counted on to pull her from her self-destruction — had that failed her too as it had failed this woman here? Had her religion completely smothered all her natural feelings?

Or had death seemed preferable to her when she found

herself abandoned and deserted and betrayed as she had been? He was sick with foreboding.

What had happened to them? They should be together. In intelligence and pride and courage they were a perfect match. With what high hopes for the future he had entered into this marriage! With what bitterness he had seen the gulf open between them, yes, and helped to widen it! With what sorrow and loneliness and regret he now beheld the shambles of their life!

What had happened to them? What madness had come over them both? Now the whole ocean was between them, and he was being sucked into the deadly vortex of imperial politics by his spiraling ambition and she was being driven headlong toward destruction by her cold, unreasoning faith!

XXI

It was three days before the games were to be held in Carthage. Since the prisoners were condemned, the special privilege of the condemned was granted to them, and foodstuffs of all kinds were brought in by their friends and relatives that their last days might be spent in feasting. In one corner of the women's cell, in which the prisoners were allowed to spend the mornings together, a large clean cloth had been laid and on it were apples, oranges, pomegranates, dates, figs, breads of all kinds, honey, sweet cakes, a dozen roasted hens, and a whole lamb. The savory smell of the roast meat and the spices filled the cell with a tantalizing aroma, the like of which they had not known in a whole month.

A table had been brought in and set in the middle of the cell that they might the better enjoy their feasting, but the abundance in the corner was as yet untouched and the table looked large and bare with only three things upon it — a round, flat loaf of bread, a small flacon of wine, and a silver cup. It was the only wine they had had in the prison since the small amount that had been allotted to the sick prisoners.

For the recently baptized Christians this was their first Mass.

The prayer that was in all their hearts this morning was the same. It was the prayer that Felicity would be brought to her time early so that they could suffer together. The thought of leaving her behind to suffer alone was a devastating one to all of them, and a crushing dread to Revocatus. Felicity herself felt such a weakness and a lack that she doubted her courage if she were deprived of the strength of her companions. How could she go on without Saturninus with his quiet humor and deep inarticulate feelings, or Saturus with his wide and vigorous optimism and his apostolic zeal, or Perpetua with her unquestioning and uncompromising courage? And Revocatus — how could she see him go? How could she stand alone?

The words of the hymn they sang caught her up in a fervor of intense petition, "Hail, gladdening light! Son of our God, giver of life alone!" "Giver of life, giver of life," Felicity prayed, "help me now; bring this life to fulfillment!"

The priest spoke to them now, not with his own words, but from his memory, for he felt humble and weak too at this time and in need of words from another to help him walk this last way. He began by recalling the words Paul wrote from prison as he waited for the headsman even as they waited now for the call to go to the arena:

"As for me, I am already poured out in sacrifice, and the time of my deliverance is at hand.

"I have fought the good fight, I have finished the course, I have kept the faith.

"For the rest, there is laid up for me a crown of justice, which the Lord, the just judge, will give to me in that day; yet not to me only, but also to all those who love his coming."

158

Saturus recalled the words of Jesus to his apostles before their commemoration of the Last Supper, words he had heard first from his grandfather who repeated them from the lips of John, words he had read over and over again until they became a part of his heart. He finished with the consoling thought:

"Amen, amen, I say to you, that you shall weep and lament, but the world shall rejoice; and you shall be sorrowful, but your sorrow shall be turned into joy.

"A woman about to give birth has sorrow because her hour has come. But when she has brought forth the child, she remembers no more the anguish for her joy that a man is born into the world.

"And you therefore have sorrow now, but I shall see you again, and your heart shall rejoice and your joy no one shall take from you."

Silently the prisoners knelt, silently they prayed, silently they poured out their hearts in adoration and petition, silently they watched the priest bless the bread and wine — "Hoc est corpus meum"; "Hic est calix sanguinis mei" — silently they received their God.

Revocatus hoped while the others prayed. He hoped that Felicity's God would answer her prayer. He hoped that he was as good and as powerful as she thought. He received Communion with the others and the bread was good and the wine sweet but he was glad when the ritual was over.

In the feasting that followed they were all relaxed and cheerful and talkative. Never had food smelled so good and tasted so delicious. Felicity seemed unusually happy, but Revocatus noticed that she ate very little. He was standing beside her, his own hunger satisfied, and he was about to ask her why she didn't eat when she became rigid and turned away from him for the space of almost a minute. When she turned back to him her smile was so wide and wonderful it made him catch his breath.

"I think it is beginning," she breathed. There was no need to explain further. He was filled with amazement and wonder at the immediate answer that had been given to her prayers.

After the feast when the men returned to their own cell Revocatus kept with him the memory of the radiance of Felicity and his awe at the visible hand of God.

❋   ❋   ❋

Throughout the afternoon Felicity walked about the cell, but she had to stop and lean against the wall when one of the pains, now deep and shuddering, came upon her. She welcomed each pain, thrilling to it, forcing the pain to become stronger, hoping so to speed up her labor. But by the end of the day she became obsessed with the fear that she would never be able to deliver, and the intensity of her fear and her agony left her shaking and almost hysterical.

Perpetua asked the jailer to send for Irene, Saturninus' wife, because she herself did not know what to do for Felicity. Her own labor had been short and with the aid of a drug administered by the midwife almost without pain or consciousness.

Irene came without delay and her warm presence reassured Perpetua, but Felicity hardly noticed her, so desperate and tense was she in her anxiety.

"You must relax, little one," Irene said, soothing her, gently stroking her brow. "The baby must come, but you won't give him a chance. I'll fix you something so that you can sleep."

160

Felicity slept then until past midnight when she awakened with a sharp and piercing pain that brought an involuntary groan from her lips. Now she could scarcely take a breath between the waves of pain that wracked her body.

❖ ❖ ❖

Revocatus did not sleep that night. He had seen Irene admitted to the cell where Felicity and Perpetua were. He could not see the cell itself from his, since they were both on the same side, though not adjacent, yet he could see all through the night a square of light coming from the small, barred window in the wooden door. He kept watch on this light, as if it would tell him something, yet it never wavered or changed. All was still and silent.

Suddenly he heard a heavy, smothered groan. He dropped to his knees and pressed his head against the door as if to be as close to Felicity as possible. And he prayed. He prayed for the first time, silently, alone. Not the *Pater noster* . . . not in Latin . . . he prayed in the dialect of his childhood, words he hadn't heard in fifteen years, words he thought he had forgotten. Words of endearment his mother had used to him, words he recalled from the play of his boyhood, with these words he addressed the suffering Christ. He knelt with Christ in the Garden of Olives and asked his pardon for the violence and anger in his life. He stood with Christ as he was scourged and crowned with thorns and begged him to accept his own scourging for his lack of faith. He walked the tortuous way of the cross with Christ and stood beneath the cross as he died. His anguish for Felicity met the anguish of the God-man and recognized it. Love acknowledged love. Through his own agony for another, he found redemption and was at last lifted to hope.

After what seemed an endless succession of hours when daylight was just beginning to filter into the cell, he heard one single, agonized scream and silence.

"Oh God," he prayed, "let me suffer now — piled up, heaped, and running over! Hold me from death, I beg you, until I have filled up this great emptiness in me with all the suffering you can give! But take her quickly, please. . . ."

He heard the high thin cry of a baby, like the faint bleating of a faraway lamb. He pressed against the door. How thick the wood and heavy the stones that kept them apart!

But not for much longer. . . .

*   *   *

Strangely enough, Felicity did not feel tired, but was filled with an elation and a peace that words cannot express. Irene bathed and swaddled the baby and held her gently, while she spoke with pity to the young mother.

"Will you let me keep her and raise her as my own, Felicity? For my loss is great too, and I will love her so, for you, for Saturninus, for the children we never had."

"Let me have her first for a minute to hold before you take her away," Felicity asked. She took the baby reverently and held her close, watching the shallow, uneven breaths that scarcely stirred the tiny body. How fragile a shell to contain such a magnificent and powerful thing — a human soul swept into this world in a great burst of reality, eternal essense spilled so generously into shape!

"Now I can truly know in advance," she whispered, "the happiness that will come after the suffering."

"But how will you be able to face death," Perpetua questioned, "when you have borne this pain with such difficulty?"

"I will never face death with courage, I know," Felicity admitted, "but only with faith. Out of this anguish has come

peace, so also out of the anguish of death there will come
even a greater peace."

For what is death if not the counterpart to this — birth?
  Heralded alike by distress of mind and body,
  An anguish pressing on the soul, an agony that
    wracks the limbs,
  Until the frightening uncertainty and pain seem
    not to be borne
  And the mind and the lips cry for release and end —
    in that unendurable instant
    life begins —
  The soul is flooded with peace,
  The eyes are opened to beauty inexpressible,
    Joy without flaw,
  Elation, God-wrought, has drawn the shade,
    sponged out the past,
  And the whole being, leaping from terror,
  Sinks, completed, into perfect peace.
For what is birth, if not in pain and ecstasy, foretaste of
  death?

Novius awaited the arrival of Vasilius in his suite at Marius' house. The ship had docked yesterday at Ostia, and he would have met him there except that the emperor required his presence. The messenger was due at any time. Novius re-filled his goblet with wine and paced about the room. He was sunk in apprehension. He wanted to hear yet he recoiled from the news. Vasilius was too late. If all had gone as he thought he would have been here two weeks ago.

Suddenly he heard the knock at the door and he opened it himself and drew Vasilius into his room, where he bade him sit and poured him wine before he would ask him his news.

"Why are you so late, Vasilius? Was the trial delayed? What took you so long? You must have known I was waiting for news."

"The trial was four weeks ago," Vasilius answered, "but I did not leave then. I stayed to see the end. I thought you would want to know everything."

"But what happened at the trial?" Novius had to ask though he feared the answer. "The priest refused to sacrifice, I'm sure, but the others — they were not even Christians yet."

"The priest baptized them and not one would sacrifice. Your wife — "

"She is not my wife," interrupted Novius, still trying to slough off the tie that neither distance nor the law had been able to dissolve.

"Vivia Perpetua," continued Vasilius, "even called down the curse of her God on Hilarion and on the emperor."

"And the sentence? What was the sentence?" Novius cried.

"They all perished in the arena on the fifteenth day of September in celebration of the birthday of Caesar Geta." It was the same day he had watched the games in Rome and experienced the harrowing premonition of her death. . . .

"All—" Novius muttered, believing, yet not believing. "Not all—all—not all?" It was a great, tortured sob rather than a question. He saw again the terrible spectacle he had beheld in the arena — the savage beasts. "No, no"—he shuddered—"not by the beasts!"

"Perpetua and the slave girl—what's her name?—they were not hurt by the beasts, just shoved a bit. They walked over to the gate. There they were quickly and mercifully dispatched by the sword."

Novius did not speak at first, trying to adjust his mind to the fact of her death—caused by him (caused by him!)—and in his anxiety to hold down his feelings of guilt, seized on the mitigating knowledge that their bodies had not been violated.

"By the sword—by the sword—it would have been instant—and painless—" Death by the sword was no stranger to a soldier.

Vasilius went on. "For the three men it was not so quick. Every beast in the amphitheater had a taste of one of them, and yet he lived. He outlasted all his companions. I never thought it was possible for one person to endure so much. And all without so much as a cry or a groan."

Novius said nothing, and Vasilius, thinking he wished more details, continued. "At first the women were brought in naked and enclosed in a net, but even the crowd cried out in horror at seeing girls so young, mothers torn from their children and shamefully exposed — "

Novius had been standing motionless during the recital by Vasilius, but at this last revelation he was suddenly seized with wild fury — at himself, at Hilarion, at everyone, but, most of all, at this senseless messenger.

"Get out!" he shouted, adding a vile epithet and turning around to look for something to hurl at the fool. The closest thing to his hand was the goblet of wine, but by the time he had seized it, the messenger had escaped through the door. The cup, so roughly handled, tipped and fell from his hands, spilling all its contents on his hands and tunic and onto the floor.

The wet coldness of the liquid shocked him from his anger and left him standing, numb and silent and alone, staring at the dark sticky stain on his tunic and the ever widening pool of red at his feet.

This story was suggested by an account written by Perpetua in prison, which has been preserved in a sixteenth-century copy in Greek and Latin. There is also a portion written by Saturus and an introduction and conclusion which some think may have been written by Tertullian.

What follows is a free translation of this document.

THE PASSION OF
SAINTS PERPETUA AND FELICITY

SINCE God is honored and men encouraged by examples of faith and the working of God's grace among the ancients, why should not modern examples also be given? For in time these modern examples will themselves become ancient, even if now they are considered of less importance. For we must not suppose in our ignorance or lack of faith that God does not work just as effectively in our times, as he promised, as he has done in the past, both to strengthen martyrs and to encourage the faithful through visions.

And so we recount these events which we know through our own experience so that those of you who were there will remember and those of you who hear it for the first time may feel a communion with the holy martyrs and through them with our Lord Jesus Christ to whom is due honor and glory for ever and ever. Amen.

Certain young catechumens were arrested, Revocatus and his fellow slave Felicitas, Saturninus, and Secundulus. Among them also well a well-born, well-educated matron, Vivia Perpetua, who was honorably married and had an infant son at the breast. She had a mother and father and two brothers, one of whom was also a catechumen. She was about twenty-two years old. What follows is the whole story of her martyrdom exactly as she wrote it with her own hand. She writes:

While I was still with my companions and my father in his affection was trying to overcome my resolution with arguments, I said, "Father. I will use an example. Do you see this vessel here — urceolum, you call it?"

He said, "I see it."

I said to him, "Could it ever be called by any other name than what it is?"

And he said, "No."

"So also I cannot be called anything other than what I am. I am a Christian."

Then my father was so enraged by that word that he threw himself against me as if he would tear out my eyes, but he only annoyed me, and he and his devil's arguments were overcome.

Then I was grateful to God to have a few days away from my father and I felt refreshed by his absence. In this time I was baptized and the Spirit moved me to ask nothing from my baptism except bodily endurance in my suffering.

After a few days we were taken to the prison and I was greatly afraid because never had I experienced such terrors. Oh dreadful day! Terrible heat because of the crowds! The roughness of the soldiers! And especially I was torn with anxiety for my baby! Then Tertius and Pomponius, holy deacons who aided us, gave money to the jailer so that after a few hours we were made more comfortable in a better part of the prison.

Then all went away and I was able to nurse my baby who had been brought to me, for he was already weak from hunger. I spoke anxiously to my mother and brother about

168

him and commended him to their care. . . . I grieved to see them grieving on my account. Such cares I suffered for many days until I gained my request that my child remain with me in prison. And at once I grew strong and was relieved of my suffering and my worry for my baby, and the prison became a palace and I would rather be there than any place else.

Then my brother said to me, "Dear sister, you are so greatly honored that you should ask for a vision that you may be shown whether you are to suffer or be released."

And since I knew that I had been favored by God with visions I promised faithfully, saying, "Tomorrow I will tell you."

So I prayed and it was shown to me in this way.

I saw a bronze ladder of marvelous size extending even to heaven, so narrow that only one person could ascend at a time. On the sides of the ladder all kinds of weapons were fixed so that anyone who went up carelessly and without looking upward would have his flesh mangled and torn by the weapons. At the base lay a dragon of amazing size who tried to frighten away those who were about to go up.

Saturus went up first. He had surrendered because of us since he had been our teacher, for when we were taken he had not been there. He came to the top and turned to me, saying, "I am waiting for you, Perpetua. See that the dragon does not bite you."

And I said, "He will not harm me, in the name of Jesus Christ," and the dragon slowly laid down his head as if in fear beneath the ladder, and using his head as the first step I climbed up.

And I saw a spacious garden and in the middle a white-haired man dressed as a shepherd milking his sheep, and many thousands of people in white garments standing about.

And he raised his head and looked at me and said, "Welcome, my child."

And he gave me some of the milk and I drank it and all those standing around said, "Amen."

At the sound of the voice I awoke, still tasting something sweet.

I told my brother and we knew that we must suffer and we began to have no hope in this life.

After a few days we heard a rumor that we would be examined. My father came from the city, weary and distressed, and tried to dissuade me, saying,

"Pity my white hair, daughter. Pity your father if I am worthy to be called a father, if I have raised you to maturity with these hands, if I have preferred you before your brothers. Consider your brothers, consider your mother. Consider your mother's sister, your son who cannot live after you are gone. Lay aside your pride. Do not destroy us all. No one of us will speak freely again if anything happens to you!"

So he spoke as a father pressing my hand in his devotion, weeping and throwing himself at my feet and speaking humbly. And I grieved for him because of all my kindred he alone would not be happy about my suffering. I tried to comfort him, saying,

"It will happen on that platform as God wills, for know that we are not in our own power but in the power of God."

And he went away saddened.

One day when we were eating our noon meal we were suddenly taken out to be examined. We came to the forum. Immediately the rumor spread to all parts of the city and an immense crowd gathered. We went up onto the platform.

The rest were questioned and declared their faith. It was now my turn.

My father came, holding my son, and he pulled me back from the steps, saying,

"Please, pity your child!"

Hilarion, the judge, who held the power of life and death since the death of the proconsul, Minucius Timinianus, said,

"Spare your father's white hair. Spare your infant son. Sacrifice for the health and safety of the emperor."

I said, "I will not."

Hilarion said, "Are you a Christian?"

I answered, "I am a Christian."

When my father continued to try to dissuade me, he was ordered by Hilarion to be pushed aside and he was struck with a rod. I grieved for my father as if I myself had been struck and I was unhappy because of his unhappiness in his old age.

Then he passed sentence on us all and condemned us to the beasts and we returned joyfully to prison.

Since my child was accustomed to staying with me in prison and nursing from me, I sent the deacon Pomponius to my father to ask for the child. But he refused. As God willed, after that my milk dried up and the child no longer needed his mother's milk so I was not distracted by anxiety for my child or my own pain. . . .

[Here follows a description of another vision Perpetua had about a brother, Dinocrates, who was no longer living.]

Then after a few days Pudens the jailer, believing we had great virtue and power, allowed many friends to visit us, and it was a great comfort to us all. When the day of the games was close at hand, my father came in great distress and be-

171

gan to tear his beard and unmindful of his age to prostrate himself and plead in a most heart-breaking manner.

The day before we were to fight I saw this in a vision.

I was brought to the middle of the arena and I seemed to have become a man. And there was an Egyptian of dreadful appearance with whom I was to fight. And when we began to fight I felt lifted up into the air and I struck him with my heels. And at last I caught hold of his head and he fell on his face and I put my foot on his head. Then I received the bough of victory.

And I awoke and I realized that I would fight not against the beasts but against the devil. But I knew that I would be victorious.

This I have written on the day before the games. If anyone wishes he may write what happened on the very day of the games.

[Here follows a lengthy vision of Saturus.]

These are the remarkable visions of the most holy martyrs Saturus and Perpetua which they wrote themselves. Secundulus God called from life earlier, not without grace that he might escape the beasts.

About Felicity it happened this way. Since she was eight months pregnant (for she was pregnant when arrested) and the day of games was drawing near, there was great sorrow lest her execution be postponed, because according to law pregnant women could not be exposed to punishment. Her fellow martyrs were much saddened at the thought of leaving such a good comrade.

So, joining in sorrow, they poured out a prayer to God on the third day before the games. And immediately after the prayer she went into labor. And since she suffered much from the natural difficulty of premature delivery, one of the warders said, "You suffer so much now. What will you do when you are thrown before the beasts?"

She answered, "Now I suffer as I must, but then there will be another who will take my suffering upon himself since I suffer for him."

She gave birth to a girl whom a Christian woman raised as her own daughter.

Now since these events were permitted by the Holy Spirit, we set them down, unworthy as we are to tell of such glory, even as we were urged to do by holy Perpetua.

On the day before the games they were allowed the special celebration given to the condemned and this they observed as a Christian love feast.

The day of their victory arrived and they proceeded from the prison into the amphitheater, as if they were on their way to heaven, joyful and cheerful, pale with elation rather than fear. Perpetua followed with clear countenance and serene bearing, as the beloved bride of Christ, and by the steadiness of her gaze put to shame the staring crowd. Felicity also, glad that she was safely delivered to fight the beasts, went from childbed to the arena, to be purified in a second baptism.

When they were led in the gate and were going to be made to put on the robes of the priests of Saturn, and the women, of the priestesses of Ceres, Perpetua, noble and constant to the end, said, "We have come here of our free will. Let not our liberty be taken away. We are giving up our lives not to do anything against our conscience. This is our agreement with you."

Injustice recognized justice, and the officer gave them permission to wear their own garments.

But he who said, "Ask and you shall receive," gave to each

one the death that he desired. For when they talked among themselves of their choice of martyrdom, Saturninus wanted to be thrown to all the beasts that his crown might be more glorious. And so also with Revocatus. [And so it happened to them.] Saturus feared nothing more than the bear but hoped to be consumed by one bite of the leopard. [His wish was granted, and Saturus was the first to die.]

A ferocious heifer had been made ready for the girls, to match their sex with that of the beast. They were brought in, stripped and enclosed in a net, but the people were horrified, seeing one a delicate girl and the other so recently from childbirth that her breasts were still dripping milk. So they were taken back and dressed in loose gowns.

First Perpetua was thrown and fell on her back. When she sat up, she pulled her tunic down, more mindful of modesty than of her pain. Then asking for a pin, she bound up her hair, thinking it not right for a martyr to suffer with hair disheveled as if in mourning. Then she rose and when she saw Felicity was injured she came and gave her her hand and helped her up and together they walked to the gate of Life.

[At first the cruelty of the crowd seemed appeased, but later they demanded they be brought back to perish by the sword. It was necessary for Perpetua herself to guide to her own throat the wavering hand of the young gladiator who dispatched them.]

O brave and blessed martyrs! Surely these modern examples of virtue testify no less than the examples of old that one and the same Spirit is working to this day with God the Father almighty and with his son Jesus Christ our Lord to whom be honor and glory without measure for ever and ever. Amen.

174